ONE WINTER IN *Door County*

CECELIA CONWAY

One Winter In Door County: Door County Dreams Book 5

Copy Editing: Novel Mechanic

Proofreader: My Brother's Editor

Cover Design and Formatting: Cruel Ink Editing + Design

AUTHOR'S NOTE

While this is a standalone, it is still interconnected with three other stories and it may be helpful to your reading experience if you read them first.

The events of the story's prologue begin right as *Three Months in Spring* are ending and the first chapters of the story begin just after Bret and Sarah from *Two Nights in August* get engaged.

Additionally, *One Winter in Door County* deals with the aftermath of the things that occurred in *Three Months In Spring.* Particularly the trial for the criminal organization that Andrea used to be involved in.

Also, Monica Price is Paul Price Jr.'s sister from the novella *Bridging the Divide,* and *One Winter* touches on the events that happened in that story.

Finally, there are potentially triggering themes and content in the book as follows

- Explicit sex on page
- Adult language
- Blackmail (not between main characters)
- Family tension
- Veterans issues (both physical and mental)

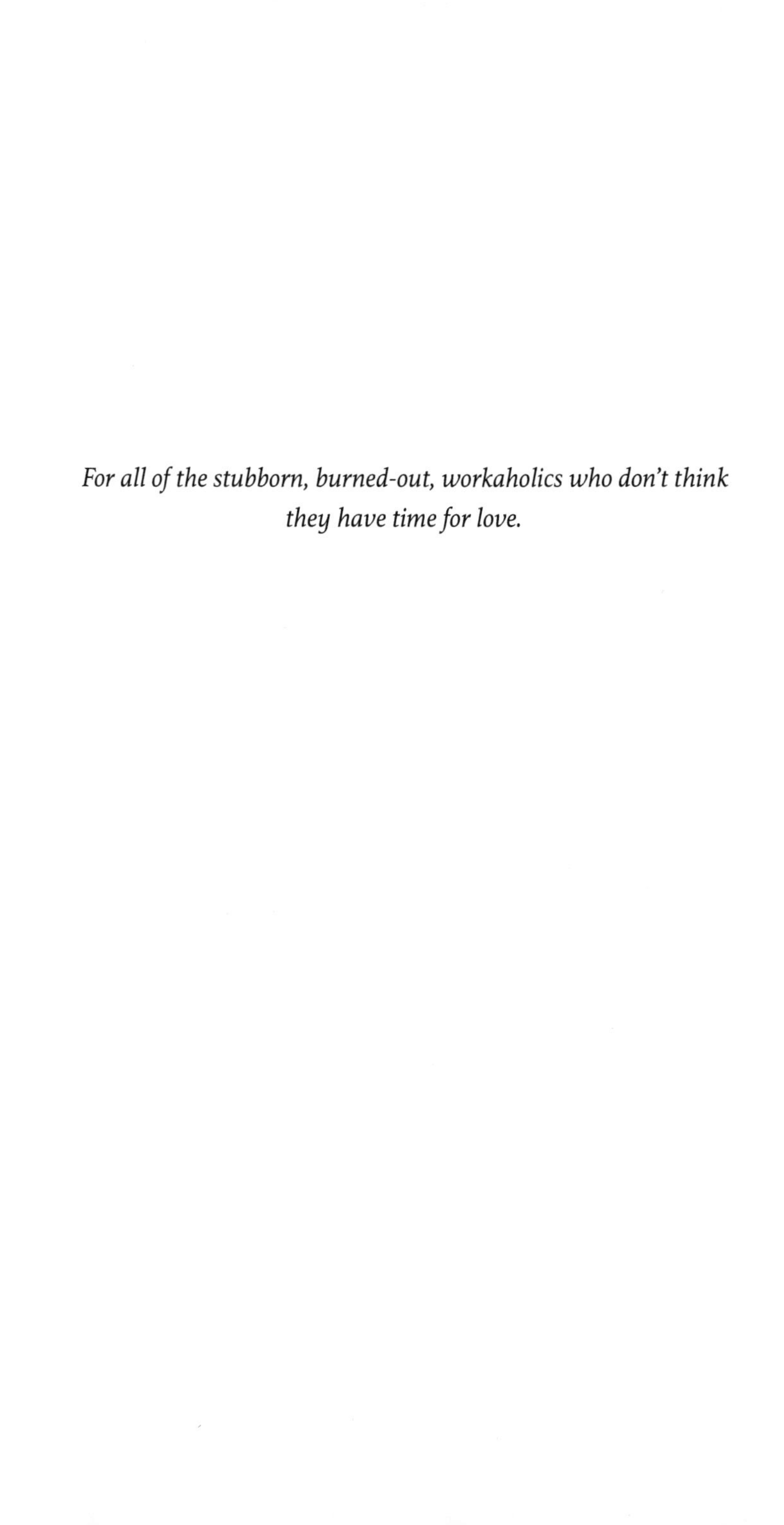

For all of the stubborn, burned-out, workaholics who don't think they have time for love.

PROLOGUE

MONICA

March

It's been a long time since I've met someone who intrigues me as much as Caleb Corcoran does. He's only an inch taller than me, maybe five-eleven, but he's wide. The tight stretch of his T-shirt highlights all the defined muscles in his chest, and a five-o'clock shadow darkens his jaw.

His presence in the room is something I can ignore. I've dealt with plenty of intimidating people as a lawyer, either my own clients or opposing counsel, but Caleb is different. Not scary or domineering. He's just there. In the few hours since we got thrust together, he's been quiet, controlled, and aloof.

Do I want him to look at me?

Yes, I think I do, but I won't let myself have a one-night stand with a virtual stranger. There's too much at risk. If my father found out, there'd be hell to pay for risking our family's reputation by looking easy. He's spent my entire life telling me how important appearances are. As a teenager, if I even thought about doing something he wouldn't approve of, all I could hear was his voice in my head chastising me.

Thank god we're in a hotel suite. It's private, and there's no chance of my dad showing up unannounced.

When Steve said Andrea wanted me to stay away from home for a little while, I didn't put up much of a fight. I've been in the loop on the case and trying to help her since she came to me, so I know how dangerous the situation is. What I didn't expect was Caleb coming with me as my pseudo-bodyguard.

Now, we're in a room with two giant beds less than ten feet away from where we're sitting, and the feeling of needing him to want me as much as I want him is all I can think about.

Shake it off, Price. He's clearly not interested.

"I've got a lot of work to do, so I'm going to go into my room for the night."

He turns and gives me a nod but doesn't stand or say anything.

The itch to make his hard exterior crack takes hold. I just want to see him bend a little. Give me any hint that he acknowledges me.

What is wrong with me? I never act like this around men.

Maybe I just need to get laid. My last serious boyfriend was just after college, and we broke up years ago. I've had a few discreet partners since, but nothing recently. I stand up and leave, shutting the door to my bedroom with a quiet click. The TV volume goes up, and I roll my eyes. We sat in awkward silence for almost an hour, him watching a silent

TV with the closed captions on while I pretended to be busy on my phone. Why didn't he just ask if he could turn the volume up?

Two can play this game. I grab my phone and turn on some music, setting it near the door so it'll sound louder than it actually is. *If he even cares what I'm doing.*

The desk is on the far side of the room, facing the window. It looks out over Green Bay, which isn't a big city like Chicago, but there are still enough people out and about that I can watch to my heart's content.

On my way over, I grab a couple of bottles from the minibar and a package of crackers. The office chair is comfortable, and I curl up, tucking my feet underneath me, pulling the blanket off the bed, and draping it over my lap.

The first bottle twists open, and I sip at it, taking my time with the stiff drink. While I snack on the crackers, I make up conversations between the people I'm watching outside. When I get bored with that, I do what I said I was going to do in the first place and open my laptop.

I'm inundated with emails I need to respond to. Our firm has been at the center of some of the most prominent cases the city has seen in the last few years, and the workload just keeps growing. It's also giving my dad a lot of ideas about what my future career plans could look like.

He was pressuring me to talk to Alana, my best friend and a current assistant district attorney, and have her give me a reference for a job in the DA's office so I could line myself up for 'career advancement.' Just the thought of that makes me want to gag, and I crack open the second bottle, downing it in one shot.

It burns going down, and I press my fist to my chest,

trying to suppress the cough that wants to explode. I'm so sick of my father's meddling, but I don't know how to stand up to him. It's not something I've thought of doing before.

The room is getting too dark to see, so I get up to turn on a lamp. On my way back, I grab three more of the mini bottles and veer toward the bed. I scoop up my laptop and earbuds, give up on work, and settle in for a movie night.

Thoughts of Caleb prod me to search for something steamier, not that I can do anything about it without risking being caught. But a girl can imagine. I skip the top search results and settle on *Secretary*. I haven't seen it before, but it looks promising.

Halfway through the movie, I hear a knock on my door. There's only one person it could be, and I flush red just thinking about what I've been watching. I leap off the bed and hastily straighten out my pencil skirt.

"Hey." I lean against the doorframe, pleasantly tipsy and still more than a little turned on by thoughts of the handsome stranger.

"Hi, I—" His eyes roam over my face and then past me, no doubt taking in the wrinkled blanket thrown across the bed and my still-open computer. At least I've been tossing out the bottles as I've finished them, so I don't look like a lush.

"What's up?" I shift and stumble a little.

He reaches out, lightning fast, and lightly holds my elbow until I'm steady. Heat churns in my stomach, and I sway toward him. "What have you been up to in here?"

The deep baritone of his voice wraps around me, and I tilt my head back, looking at him with more brazenness than I feel. "Why don't you come in and see?"

To my shock, he steps inside and lets the door shut

behind him. I fumble for the light switch. Some instinct for self-preservation wants to hide in the darkness if this doesn't turn out like my lady parts are hoping it will.

I can feel Caleb's eyes bore into my back as I go to the fridge and pull out the last four bottles. Then, deciding to be brave, I take his hand and lead him to the bed, pointing to the side without the crushed pillows. If he rejects me, at least I'll have my comfy little nest already arranged.

His eyes lock on my computer screen, and I pull out my earbuds so he can hear it. He toes his shoes off and climbs on the bed. I hand him two of the liquor bottles and settle the blanket back across my lap, nerves making my fingers shake.

We watch together, inches apart but not touching. I can feel the heat radiating off of him, and at some point, I shuck off the blanket, squirming to ease the ache building between my legs.

His fingers twitch toward me, but he holds himself rigidly back. I can hear his breathing speed up when we get to the spicy bits, and I can't help but match it. Needing some modicum of control, I don't reach toward him. He needs to make the first move.

Good god, just touch me! I scream the words in my head, trying to catch his reaction out of the corner of my eye.

The credits roll, and he reaches out to shut the computer, picking it up and carefully setting it on the bedside table. I watch him, noticing the tent in his pants and smiling at the proof that he's not unaffected.

He turns back toward me and pauses. The bed lamp is still on, so it's not completely dark, and I see how his pupils have blown wide. "Why did you show me this?"

Be brave. Tell him what you want. "I'm very attracted to

you." I turn to face him on my knees. "And I swear I never do this."

"Do what?" His voice sounds strained, and his hands clench into fists.

My fingers trail up the center of my body, tracing the line of buttons until I reach the top one. One by one, I ease them free. His gaze sears me, but it feels encouraging. Before I get the last one undone, he lunges, and we fall to the bed in a tangle of limbs.

When I wake up in the morning, I'm alone, and there isn't a noise in the suite. I assume Caleb must have gone back to his room at some point, but I think little of it. We were both tipsy and horny and didn't really talk much beyond that. Waking up together would have only been more awkward.

I roll out of bed and stretch, pleasantly sore and thoroughly satisfied. Even if he thinks last night was a mistake, I don't regret it. A hot shower is just what I need to wake up and chase away the mild hangover from drinking more than I usually do.

I'm midway through toweling off when I get a call from my brother. Since he's not great about reaching out in person regularly, I settle on the edge of the counter and answer. "What's up?"

We make small talk for a bit before he gets to the real reason he called, and I take a few minutes to give him the legal advice he's looking for. I can't shake the feeling that he's tired and ready to stop serving in the state legislature. Like my father, my brother ran for public office. Unlike my father, my brother isn't cut out for it. He did it because it was expected of him, but I've seen how cynical he's become. Paul's always tired and cranky, but now I can hear the glimmer of happiness when he talks about opening up his own firm.

I couldn't be happier for him.

After hanging up, I throw on some casual clothes and wander out into the living area to see if Caleb is up yet. I don't see him and don't want to wait to eat, so I order room service, making sure there's extra for him.

He finally comes out of his room when he hears the knock on the door, signaling the food's arrival. His expression is alert, intense, and focused, and I get a glimpse of why he's here. Without hesitating, I step back and let him go to the door and accept the food.

"You should have let me know someone was coming up." His tone is terse, and it immediately pisses me off.

"I would have if you hadn't been hiding in your room. It's obvious you've been up for a while." He's dressed, and there's not a trace of sleepiness about him.

He grumbles but says nothing else. We eat in tense silence that sets the tone for the rest of the day. Our personalities clash over little things, and we start taking potshots at each other. Everything comes to a head when I get a text from Alana begging for help.

Please help. Can't call, but someone's here. I think it might be the same people who were shooting at us before.

Alana was out dancing with us when one of Andrea's old enemies shot at us outside of a bar a few weeks ago.

I'm calling the police, and I'm on my way.

My response is automatic and without hesitation. I grab

my purse and keys and head for the door without a second thought.

"Where are you going?" Caleb barks, jogging after me and blocking the door.

"We have to go. Alana's in trouble." My fingers are already moving over the keypad to dial nine-one-one.

"No. We'll call the police and let them take care of it."

I jab a finger into his chest. "I'm going." Caleb crosses his arms and plants his feet. Without thinking twice about it, I knee him in the balls and rush past, running toward the stairs, not wanting to wait for the elevator.

"Goddamn it," he wheezes but chases after me. I dial quickly.

When we reach my car, he tries to take the keys from me, but I glare and rip open the driver's side door. "Get out of my way or get in over there."

He doesn't move, but I'm not waiting, so I climb in and gun the engine. Before I put it in gear, he clambers into the passenger's side, and I back out, speeding out of the parking area and onto the street.

Alana lives outside of town, so I rush toward the highway. Caleb's pissed, but I don't care. "If people are going after your friend, what do you think you're going to do?"

"Are you telling me you'd just sit at home if your friends were in trouble?" He may be a jerk, but I know he cares about Matt and Steve.

"What I wouldn't do is rush into a dangerous situation with no way of protecting myself!" His deep voice is commanding, and I feel a twinge of worry that I'm doing something stupid, but I push it down. The on-ramp is coming up, and I signal for it, easing the car into the turn lane with slightly less speed than before.

"I called the cops." Everything is becoming too overwhelming, and I just don't know how to feel or what to do. Suddenly, all I want to do is cry. I accelerate onto the highway and try to ignore him.

"Don't get hysterical on me now." He reaches over and puts his hand on my knee. It's strangely comforting, and I give him a small smile. "Why don't we think about this a little more? You can pull over at the next exit, I'll drive, and we'll let the cops do their job."

I shake my knee to dislodge his hand. "No." All my good feelings evaporate.

"For god's sake, listen to reason."

And that's when we're rear-ended. My car goes spinning out of my control. Thankfully, there's not much traffic, and I don't hit anyone else. My poor Lexus slams into the concrete dividing wall, and my head whips forward, smacking into the steering wheel.

Ringing fills my ears, and I feel dizzy. A car slows as it goes by us and pulls over. The driver gets out and runs over. I can barely make out their features and can't tell what they're saying. They go to Caleb's side of the car and tap on the window.

I hear them saying something, and I think they have a cell phone out. Hopefully, they're calling an ambulance.

Oh god, I need to puke.

My fingers scramble for the door handle, but when I push, it doesn't open. Feeling around, I try to find the window button, but that doesn't work either.

"Breathe. Through your nose." Caleb's voice cuts through the ringing, and I finally notice the way he's running his hands over me, checking to see if I'm injured. "You're okay. Just breathe."

He sounds scared. Should I be scared?

"They've got an ambulance coming. Whoever hit us took off. You're okay."

Someone hit us on purpose?

It's the last thing I think before I pass out.

PROLOGUE

CALEB

Halloween

Monica Price is a conglomeration of everything that pisses me off in a person. She's attention-seeking, two-faced, and overly ambitious. It doesn't help that she's an exceptional liar who makes you believe what she's telling you despite every instinct telling you to run.

But I have to put those feelings aside tonight because we're celebrating our friends' engagement, and I want things to be civil. If my feelings get the better of me, then Monica and I will wind up yelling at each other, and I'll never forgive myself. Tonight is about Sarah and Bret—celebrating their engagement and throwing an enormous party for Andrea and Steve's new place.

I'm lucky they're all still willing to invite me. These last few years have been difficult, and I haven't made it easy to be my friend. Between isolating myself after the accident and throwing all of my time and energy toward starting the bed-and-breakfast, I've been markedly absent.

Across the room, Monica's standing as far away from me as possible. Which is fine. It gives me even less reason to look at her or have to pretend to make small talk.

"Come on. It's almost time," Andrea whisper-shouts and herds the group closer to the door so we can cheer on Bret and Sarah when she says yes. There's no doubt about her answer. The two of them are madly in love with each other. Too bad it took them almost a year to admit it.

Matt puts his arm around Nore's shoulders and kisses the top of her head, smiling down at her with a sappy look. She snuggles into his side and wraps her arm around his waist. The picture of a happy couple. Even Steve is trying to dote on Andrea as much as she'll let him. The two of them have divergent personalities, but they fit together like two halves of a whole.

It seems like all my friends have found their person this year. I should be envious, but I'm happy for them. They're all good men, and the women they've fallen in love with are just what they need.

And while they've been settling into steady relationships, I'm turning into a full-blown recluse, remote lighthouse included. Even though I was planning on renting it, it's still isolated from most of the larger surrounding towns. During the off-season, I get to ramble around without running into anyone. Since I got discharged from the Army, I've had a hard time trusting new people. The closest friend I've made is Sherman, the grumpy stray cat who's lived on the property longer than I have.

I was different when I was enlisted. It was easy to become close friends with the men and women in my unit, and we still stayed in touch, but most of them are still active and deployed overseas.

Clapping and happy laughter echo around the space, making me flinch and realize I've missed the entire proposal while I zoned out. Sarah and Bret are grinning at each other in the entranceway of the greenhouse. Even from this far away, I see the sparkling rock he must have just slipped onto her finger. The only thing brighter in the room is Sarah's smile.

I try to tell myself that it's curiosity that makes me seek out Monica. She's smiling just as widely as anyone else, clapping and yelling congratulations. The part that makes my gut twist with a sick combination of envy and anger is that she looks genuine.

Amazingly, she doesn't have a photographer here taking pictures. The bitter thought slithers through my mind. She's probably well-trained by her father to collect photographic evidence to use for good PR later. After all, he is the great Paul Price Senior.

The willpower it takes to rip my eyes away from her when she turns her head toward me is disconcerting. *Clap. Smile. Act like a human.* I have to remind myself that this is what normal people do in these situations. Not gawk at the infuriating woman across the room.

Steve steps up next to me and leans close so I can hear him over the noise. "Andrea told me to tell you if you need a break tonight, the restaurant is unlocked. Go over there whenever you need to."

Relief ripples through me. When I got the invitation for a Halloween party, my response was an automatic no. Noise and people make me feel claustrophobic, and my friends would understand why I didn't want to be there. But then I caught wind of what Bret was planning and knew I needed to come. Having the small escape of going over to the restaurant is a godsend.

"Tell her thanks. The place looks great, by the way." Steve and Andrea have been working nonstop to get everything back up and running after the fire this past spring.

"Thank you. We're excited about how it's all coming together." His eyes find Andrea in the crowd and linger on her. They're always checking in with each other in an unspoken language that's exclusive to the two of them. "Andrea's the genius behind it. I just do her organizing." He grins and drifts back toward her before they both move to a corner, conferring with the servers about something.

The crowd mobs Bret and Sarah, so I hang back, noting with another unwilling look her way that Monica is doing the same thing. There are still twenty minutes before the public starts showing up, and I give myself a mental kick in the butt. I've got to make it until then so I don't look like a terrible person. No one would expect me to stay much longer than that, even with the escape route Andrea's given me.

While I wait for an opportunity to congratulate Bret and Sarah, I grab a drink from the open bar. The ice cubes swirl in the soda, leaving trails of bubbles in their wake. My mind focuses on watching the random patterns instead of fixating on the surrounding noise. Little by little, the feeling of being overwhelmed ebbs away.

When I glance around the room, I spot Al and Annie laughing together at one of the far tables. Steve and Andrea are bustling back and forth from the service area, making sure everything is ready for when the crowd arrives. Only Matt and Lenore linger near Sarah and Bret.

I make my way toward them, slipping past people I don't recognize. A nodded greeting keeps me moving without giving anyone an opening to talk to me. Before I can make it to Bret and Sarah, more people converge on them. I detour to the edge of the room, finding a place where I can watch for another opportunity.

Even before everything happened, I wasn't much of a party or people person. Which is ironic because I now own a bed-and-breakfast. Ever since I was a little kid, I've wanted to own that property. My parents took me there on one of our few family outings, so it's always been a bright spot in my memories. Turning it into a B and B is the easiest way to make the property pay for itself, and I know if I do it right, I'll be able to make a living.

My mind drifts to everything I'll have to get done over the winter to prepare for the summer tourist season. I've had a few people come and stay this year, mostly friends or friends of friends, as test runs to get a basic idea of how well things ran and get some feedback, but I haven't opened it to the public yet.

Next summer would be my first full season in business. I have enough savings to be comfortable this winter, but if I don't at least break even next year, I'll be in trouble. Repairs are costing more than I expected, even doing most of the work myself.

On top of all the maintenance, the business aspects need to be taken care of: permits, state inspections, insurance, and advertising. Nore promised to head up the advertising and gave me her "friends and family" discount. All she asked was that I let her use it as a sample for her growing portfolio.

Across the room, Monica catches my eye. Like me, she

seems out of place at this party. At least I bothered to put together a costume. If a tool belt and flannel shirt counted as one. It didn't look like she changed from work, so her well-tailored black suit stood out like a sore thumb amid everyone else's colorful choices.

She looks good in a suit, though. Even I can't deny that.

My mind flashes back to last spring and watching her take off that suit and the matching set of bra and panties underneath. And everything that happened after.

I stick a finger under my collar and tug, reminding myself that whatever I thought we had between us is long gone. Between my guilt over the car accident to the shit she said at the hospital when she didn't think anyone was listening, there wasn't any chance of a second round.

I shake my head, tearing my gaze away and shutting down any attraction that might still be festering.

Monica Price is not someone I intend to re-familiarize myself with in any sense of the word. The few days I was stuck with her this spring showed me just how easy it was for her to put on a show for her friends. The real Monica Price hides behind a thick mask she rarely lets slip.

Is it too early to go home?

I make my way around the room, nodding and saying my goodbyes to everyone. It's getting more crowded now, so my absence won't be noticed. If I'm lucky, I'll be able to catch a word with Sarah and Bret on the way out. Otherwise, I'll swing by their house next week and give my congratulations.

"Are you trying to sneak away already?" Her voice is sharp and distinct, and my back straightens defensively.

"I don't sneak." I also don't bother turning around to face her. "That's all you."

She walks in front of me so we're facing each other. "That's rich coming from you. You're good at sneaking away from actually feeling anything."

I barely contain the wince. That barb hits close to home. "At least I don't buy my friends."

It's fascinating to watch her face flush with fury. With everyone else, she's a cool mask of polite friendliness, but I seem to be the only person who can make her lose control. A small part of me feels bad for sinking to her level, but I reacted before I thought things through.

"You are such an asshole. I thought, tonight of all nights, you'd at least try."

"I'm here, aren't I?" I spread my hands wide.

"We're not doing this here." She grabs my wrist and hauls me to the greenhouse. Now that everyone's inside the banquet hall, the greenhouse is dark and empty.

I should have come out here earlier.

Monica's fierce grip catches me off guard enough that I follow without resistance. She keeps us moving until we're shrouded in the farthest corner, behind a Halloween display the florist set up, and in the shadow of one of the tall storage cabinets.

When she stops and turns to face me, I smirk, knowing that she'll take it as a challenge. The one thing I still enjoy about our interactions is the way she always rises to the bait. Monica Price isn't one to back down from a fight.

Just like I knew she would, she straightens to her full height and lifts her chin. "I would have thought you'd at least try to be supportive of your friends, but you're not even the type of man who can do that, are you? Why am I even bothering to get upset about this?" I know I've been an ass when we've run into each other through our mutual friends and their get-togethers, but she still has the power to make me feel small.

She looks down at her feet when she's finished. The moonlight coming through the clear roof makes her dark hair shine and dance when she shakes her head in an infinitesimal movement. To my surprise, she stops berating me and turns away. I don't know why, but I reach out and grab her arm, keeping her here with me. "Since when do you run away from an argument?"

I don't like the defeat in her shoulders or the way everything about her is deflating before my eyes. To me, it's clear she's decided I'm not worth the effort.

"I'm smart enough to recognize arguing with you. It does me no good if it won't change the outcome." Even in the dark, I can sense her eyes on me, studying my face like she needs another reason to stay. "No need to make a fool of myself."

She pulls her arm from my grip and goes back to the party. I replay the conversation, thinking about the way her expression changed with each word she said and trying to pinpoint the exact moment she'd lost hope in me.

An uncomfortable feeling swells low in my stomach. Dread or some other nameless emotion that I don't want to think about at the moment.

I stand where she left me. My brain's fixated on the fact that Monica Price thinks so little of me.

And I feel a singular drive to prove to her that I am worth the effort.

1

CALEB

I haven't been able to get a full night's sleep since Halloween, not that I was getting much before that. All my usual worries are amplified. Money. Insurance. Business. Property ownership. Monica Price.

When I fall asleep, my brain conjures up visions of all the worst things that could happen, and it's deeply disturbing how often Monica plays a starring role. No matter what I do, I can't stop thinking about her.

Even though it's mid-November, I rarely sleep with covers on. I've woken up too many times with them tangled around me, thrown into even more of a fight-or-flight mode than my nightmares could do.

Sherman's glowing yellow eyes peer at me, judgment clear on his squashed face. The previous owner told me he'd been hanging around for a few years but never wanted to go inside. It was just my luck that he turned up on my porch a few days after I moved in and decided he wanted a house to live in. I took pity on the huge, matted goon and got him some food. Slowly but surely, he went back to looking and acting like a normal cat.

He had to be some sort of Persian cross because of his smushed-in face and permanent frown, with none of the wheezy breathing issues that were common among the breed. After it became clear that he was adopting me, I did some research and assumed caregiving duties to the best of my ability.

"Might as well get up and do something," I tell him. The only response I get is a slow blink.

Swinging out of bed, I stretch, cracking my back and wincing when my feet make contact with the cool wood floor. One of these days, I'll get around to finding a rug that will fit in the room, but that's not a necessity right now. I've certainly slept in worse conditions, and those were some of the last nights I got adequate sleep.

My doctor keeps talking to me about sleep meds, but I'm adamant about not using them. I wanted to at least try something natural, like melatonin or aromatherapy, but I was lucky if they worked for more than a day or two.

Sherman's eyes track my movements, but nothing else on his body moves. It's eerie, and I eye him for a second before getting dressed. "Be good, gremlin. I'll get your breakfast ready by the usual time."

His eyes close, and he lowers his head, content that he's sufficiently trained me to his high standards.

By habit, I start my day even though it's not even four in the morning. Between my to-do list, finishing winterizing the place, and the computer work I still need to get caught up on, I can keep myself busy for most of the day.

After making sure that Sherman's food is out and in the bowl he prefers, I tug on my coat and trudge outside, heading for the storage shed where I've been keeping all of my extra supplies for the guest house.

By the time I make it back to the house, it's well after dark. Sherman's waiting for me in the front window of the cabin, staring with contempt because his dinner is late.

I'm bone tired and should be mentally exhausted, but my mind is still spinning.

After I feed myself and Sherman, I check my voicemail, listening to a message from the therapist I got a referral for. Making a note of the appointment on my calendar, I lean back in my office chair.

Time to bust out the accounting work and see if that might put me to sleep.

IT'S two in the morning when I struggle out of a nightmare. All my worries swirled together and attacked again, sending me into a sweating, writhing mass of limbs on the bed. Not even Sherman stayed with me. When my mind clears enough to focus, I spot him curled up on the chair across the room, his tail disdainfully draped over his face.

With too much force, I rub the heel of my palms into my eye sockets. I feel used up and hollowed out inside.

The muted TV is still on, and the sleep timer I scheduled to turn it off not having kicked in yet. I stack up some pillows behind my head and reach for the remote. No use in trying to go back to sleep, and I need something to chase the images out of my head. Especially the last one that woke me up.

Monica Price, walking away from me yet again.

2

MONICA

These last few months have been tricky, and I've been walking a fine line between getting too involved and just supporting my coworkers as they gather materials for the civil trial against The Organization. Since I was indirectly involved because of what happened in the spring with Andrea, I've been told to "work on other cases to help lighten the load." No one wants to risk the results of the trial, including me, so I've been taking on the overflow from everyone else.

Mostly, I've been trying to stay out of it, except my father is breathing down my neck. He keeps pushing me to get more involved because he thinks it could be the type of public relations win that will set me up for an assistant district attorney position and then, in a few years, the district attorney's seat. Then a few more years after that, either a judgeship or a position higher up in government. The first step is taking Alana's old job as an ADA. Alana, who is on trial for conspiracy and a host of other charges.

Alana, who I thought was my closest friend.

Thankfully, the women I met before everything happened—Lenore, Sarah, and Andrea—haven't let me hide away in my apartment and let myself be consumed by work. They've grown from being clients to stanch friends, and for that, I'm grateful.

That's why Caleb's words at the Halloween party stung so badly. I had a hard enough time making friends that I was well aware of the privilege these women give me. They've never judged me and never tried to get close to me just because of my last name. They're real and kind, and I'd do anything for them.

Since the Halloween party, I've been doing my best to extinguish all thoughts of that frustrating man. I felt a spark of connection with him back in the spring when Andrea and Steve arranged for him to come and keep an eye on me, but everything flamed out so fast that even I still wasn't sure what had happened.

There'd been that one night, but it never happened again.

Thank god.

Caleb is insufferable. Bossy. Introverted to the point of being a recluse. A homebody who looks more like a mountain man than the owner of an up-and-coming bed-and-breakfast. I'd glimpsed some of the promo materials Nore was mocking up, and they were impressive.

"Monica. Here are more files for you to go over." Our office's paralegal, Alicia, hauls in a paper box that's almost overflowing.

"Thank you. Can you put it on the chair for now?" Since I've been taking over more of our pro bono and contract cases, I've had less and less use for my visitor chair.

"Sure thing. You need anything else?" She's a sweet girl,

just out of community college and trying to decide if she wants to keep going after her paralegal certification and pursue her law degree. I've been mentoring her for a year now, and I'm enjoying seeing her confidence and knowledge grow with every case we work on.

"Not right now. Thank you, though. Did you get your lunch yet?" I feel bad for foisting my work ethic on her. Some days, she skips lunch and stays as late as I do.

"I was hoping I could take it now, if that's alright? My mom's in town, and we were going to grab a bite."

"Of course. Take all the time you need. You've earned it." She's going to make an excellent lawyer if she goes back to school. I'm not sure what's holding her back, but I'll find out eventually.

"Thanks, Miss Price. I really appreciate it."

She closes the door behind her, leaving me once again with my computer and reams of papers to go over.

IT'S WELL past dusk when I pack my things and leave the office. Everyone else went home to their families hours ago, but I stayed, trying to minimize the time I spent alone in my apartment.

My eyes are dry and scratchy from staring at a screen too long. Even when I try to take breaks, I have all the files that Alicia dropped off with their fine print and my chicken scratch notes. It feels like my shoes are made of lead as I pick my way down the snow-covered sidewalk to our parking lot, situated between a handful of other local businesses. I have to concentrate on each step when the pavement's icy because the last thing I want is to slip on a patch of ice and land on my ass.

Early December isn't usually this snowy, but it's been an early year for winter storms.

I started my car before I left the office door, so it's just getting to that pleasantly warm stage by the time I open the door. My body sags into the driver's seat, and I groan as the heat seeps into my stiff muscles. Lethargy pulls me into a half-awake state, and I shake it off, focusing instead on the short drive to my apartment.

When I reach my building, I pull into my parking spot and sigh, leaning my head against my hands on the wheel. Sleep is still trying to convince me to close my eyes, so I drag myself upright, grab my bag, and head up to my third-floor apartment.

The halls are quiet, and the lights have already dimmed because it's so late. Twice, my key misses the lock, and I have to concentrate to get it lined up just right. The lights are on, and the radio is playing softly, thanks to the built-in smart home systems that came with the apartment.

Bone tired, it's all I can do to lock the door and throw myself on the bed. I don't think twice about wrinkling my clothes, already being pulled under by sleep.

In the morning, the whine of my alarm wakes me up with a jolt. I slept fitfully, the memories of the car accident meshing together with the shooting, Alana's betrayal, and Caleb's sudden cold shoulder. Everything that sent my life swerving out of control these last six months revisits me when I close my eyes.

Groping for my phone, I hit the dismiss button and peer at the screen. My battery is dangerously low, so I put it on the charger before hauling myself up to shower away yesterday.

I know I need to take better care of myself, and it wouldn't hurt to see a therapist, but if my father ever found out, he'd throw a fit and tell me to stop going because it would show that I was weak. Mom might be more understanding, but in the end, Dad was more stubborn and got what he wanted.

Despite the way he makes me feel like a puppet he's controlling most of the time, I still care about what he thinks of me. Mom's tried to get me to just ignore his comments and meddling, but they always seem to stick like a splinter just under my skin. After getting ready, I arrive at the office exactly when I'm supposed to and get a coffee from the reception area. No one knows how late I stay, but they notice if I'm here before anyone else. I try to fly under the radar and pretend that everything is okay. That I've still got my shit together. The day passes in a blur of meetings, calls, and a never-ending pile of papers to go through.

When the clock on my desk ticks over to five, I force myself to gather my things. Last week, Dad made it clear that I'm expected for dinner tonight, no doubt so he can work on ensuring my cooperation with his plans for my career.

That or complain about Paul.

There are a few shocked looks when I step out of my office with my coat on, ready to leave with everyone else. I ignore them and hurry out the door. The family is converging at my grandmother's house, almost an hour outside of Green Bay. She purchased a "cabin" in the country when she retired, and my dad prefers to conduct family-related business there since it's private and far away from prying eyes. Halfway there, my eyes drift closed, exhaustion creeping up on me again. I turn up the radio and find an annoying station to sing along with at the top of my lungs. My off-key rendition of a pop hit will keep me awake more than my usual legal podcasts do.

I'm fifteen minutes away from Grandma's house when my eyes drift lower, despite my halfhearted singing. The tires slowly ease out of the driving lane and onto the snow-slick shoulder. When the car slides, I jerk to alertness, over-correcting and sending myself spinning sideways into the oncoming lane.

Forcing myself to stay calm, I correct the skid and stop before I'm off the pavement. Thankfully, this is a country road with a lot less traffic, so I put the car in park and give myself a second to get my wits back together.

A glimmer of oncoming headlights knocks me out of my shocked stupor, and I shift back into drive, taking the rest of the way much more slowly than I was before.

The radio is still blaring, but instead of helping me stay awake, it's giving me a pounding migraine, which is the last thing I need before dealing with my father. At least Mom and Grandma will be there to help keep him in line. I jab my finger at the mute button, and the speakers fall silent.

Paul and Lisa were supposed to come up, but developments with their healthcare reform bill are keeping them in Madison. Lucky break for them. Unfortunately for me, that means I'll have to listen to Dad's jabs at him behind his back.

I hate family dinners without my brother. My soon-to-be sister-in-law is also becoming a fast ally at each skirmish.

For someone with a reputation for being a hothead, she's remarkably good at dealing with my father's meddling.

I take ten minutes longer than it should to get to Grandma's and earn myself a suspicious look from her when I walk in the front door. Mom's in the study on the phone, talking to what sounds like one of her nurses if the medical lingo flying around is anything to go by.

"Come with me. I need some help in the kitchen," Grandma says by way of greeting. She's pretty much my favorite person in the world, so I follow her without question, knowing that she doesn't really need help. She's just buying me some extra time away from my dad.

"Your ploys are lacking in subtlety these days." I smile and lean against the counter.

"Then maybe you should come out to visit more often so I can practice." She raises an eyebrow and pours me a glass of wine. "What happened?"

I take a slow sip of the wine, hiding my face behind the enormous glass. "Nothing. Why?"

"Monica Ann Price, do not lie to me." Her voice is sharper than I've heard in a long time. *God, I must look worse than I think.*

"I hit a patch of ice on the way here and scared myself. Just got a little rattled, that's all."

Her gray eyes study me, lips pursed. "There's more than that."

She always could see through me, even as a child. "Too much to talk about tonight."

I get a nod of understanding and a change of subject. "Your father is on a call, so you've got a few minutes."

Relief courses through me at the longer reprieve. "How have you been? I'm sorry I haven't been out in a while."

"Fit as a fiddle." She pulls a pair of mitts on and busies herself with whatever's on the baking tray in the oven. "Haven't felt this great in years. With the wedding to look forward to and Christmas right around the corner, I feel ten years younger."

Paul and Lisa are planning to get married sometime over the summer, but preparations are already in full swing.

Mom comes into the kitchen, her steps slowed by whatever patient she's still thinking about. "Hello, dear." She wraps me in a hug when she gets to the counter next to me, and I hug her back, lingering in the warm, familiar—slightly antiseptic—scent of Mom.

"Hi, Mom."

She steps back, keeping her hands on my shoulders and studying my face. "You haven't been sleeping again, have you?"

I've struggled with insomnia since I was little, but all the stress from work is making it worse than usual. "A lot is going on at work right now."

She squints like she knows that's not the whole truth but lets it go without pressing.

"You ladies want to set the table? I thought we'd use the Christmas plates." Grandma looks torn. Her "just in case""is left unsaid. In our family, Christmas doesn't always happen with all of us together, and Paul's already said he's spending the holiday with Lisa's family this year.

Mom and I set five places at the table. Grandma still insists we leave the spot open at the head of the table for Grandpa, and I pay special attention to that one, ensuring everything is in place. A little nudge gets the plate to the exact center of the placemat, and I line the utensils so they're perpendicular to the edge of the table. The routine of doing this these last few years helps me feel settled.

Dad comes down from upstairs before we finish and studies the table. "We should take some pictures so we can post them later." Looks like he's already got other plans for Christmas that he hasn't told us about. Mom glares at him but doesn't protest. After spending forty years as a politician's wife, she's used to his staged photo ops.

"Monica. A word." He motions to the living room, and I lead the way. It's best to go along with whatever he wants to say, nodding and smiling until you can escape.

While I settle into an armchair and brace myself for battle, Dad goes to the bar and pours two drinks. He hands me one, but I don't touch it since I already have the glass of wine waiting in the kitchen. I'm going to have to drive home tonight, and with my constant exhaustion, it's already going to be riskier than usual.

"We need to file paperwork soon so we can get started on the campaign to fill your brother's seat." He sips his drink, watching me over the rim of the glass. Like he knows I'm going to object and is just waiting for me to make a scene.

Despite the fact that he thinks I'm the black sheep of the family for not following in his footsteps, I don't enjoy fighting with him. What I do like are semi-normal family dinners, which means tonight isn't the night I'm going to argue with him. "Can't it wait until after Christmas, at least? Or the new year?"

"We'd miss an important window for fundraising."

I sigh. He doesn't want to hear it, but we could finance a campaign ourselves without having to worry about gathering donors.

"I know you're reluctant to do this." He sounds almost human for once. "But it's part of our family legacy. Especially since Paul is abandoning it to go open his own firm." He sips more of the drink. "It's this or the district attorney's track you've already been dragging your feet about. Toughen up, girl. If you want to be successful, sometimes you have to call in favors even when you don't want to."

This has been his ultimatum for the last few months, and he knows I'll never pursue Paul's seat in the state senate. However, the thought of taking Alana's old job as an assistant district attorney is equally unpalatable. Just thinking of Alana sours my mood and sends me into a spiral of sadness. "Let's go have dinner. I promise I'll think more about it."

"Don't stall. Time is of the essence. Especially with trial preparations in full swing." He leads the way out to the dining room, where Mom and Grandma are just setting out all the food.

Despite my efforts not to start a fight, dinner is stilted. I sit between Mom and Grandma, doing my best to avoid Dad's pointed looks and help Grandma try to move the conversation along. By the time I'm finally able to leave, a throbbing headache is circling my head. I pop a couple of painkillers and make my way home.

"Monica, can you come to my office for a moment?" My eyes are burning from a lack of sleep and the lingering remnants of last night's migraine poking at my brain. Disquiet roils my stomach. There's no happy outcome when those words come out of one of the firm's partners. Especially when she has that look on her face.

"Of course." I stand and smooth my skirt, trying to be subtle about slipping my heels back on before I step out from behind my desk. I follow Naia back to her office, where she sits in one of the two guest chairs, motioning for me to take the other.

Shit.

"Monica. Please know that this is not me giving you a formal reprimand."

Double shit.

"We're concerned about you."

"I—" Words and thoughts jumble in my head until I'm frozen in uncertainty, not sure what to say or do to fix whatever is wrong.

Naia reaches out and lays a hand on my knee, patting it with reassurance. "You are an excellent lawyer, and you've been doing phenomenal work these last few months while we get everything sorted out with the civil case against Alana and the other members of The Organization."

I sense a but coming.

"Lately, we've had some concerns." She pulls a file from the desk that's thicker than I would have ever imagined. "There have been some inconsistencies in your work, especially the court cases. Basic elements are being missed, or things aren't getting turned in on time. Your contracts are beyond reproach, so we're not sure what's going on."

"Mistakes?" Casework was the focus of most lawyers' careers, but contracts are my bread and butter, one of my favorite parts of law. I loved trying to think of all the loopholes and contingencies that might be needed in each unique situation. But, since the firm primarily specializes in defense and criminal injury, I've become a jack-of-all-trades and picked those up too.

Naia sighs. "Typos, assumptions that don't connect with evidence, minor inconsistencies. Things like that. Let me stress we are not concerned about that. We're concerned about you."

An inarticulate sound of question and confusion escapes before I can suppress it.

She takes my hand between hers. I can't peel my gaze away from her deep brown eyes and the sincere concern there. "Are you okay? These last few months have been a lot for all of us, but especially you."

My mouth opens and closes like a fish, and all I can do is shake my head no. To my shame, tears well in my eyes. I duck my head so she won't see me losing control.

"Oh, honey." She leans forward and wraps me up in a hug. My chest heaves, but I force the tears to stay back. I'm not doing this in front of one of my bosses.

"I am so sorry." I pull back after a few moments.

She gives me a kind smile that makes me relax. "Me too. This next part may come off a little harsh, but we believe it's for the greater good."

Triple shit.

"We're placing you on a leave of absence. At least for a month, but longer if you need it. We can discuss your return to work after New Year's and what that might look like."

My whole body freezes in horror. "What?" My words are sharper and louder than I mean them to be, but Naia doesn't react; she just keeps her soft smile in place.

"Take this time to regroup. Unwind. We all have faith in your future, but you won't do anyone any good if you burn out before you turn thirty. You'll still get paid, so no need to worry about that."

My neurons fire up, trying to conjure up an argument against their declaration.

"This decision is effective immediately. Go home, Monica. Get some sleep. If you'd like, I can give you the number of a good therapist as well. I've been seeing her for years."

Numbness seeps through me, and I stand with a lurch. "I. . . I'll be in touch." I don't have the energy to fight right now. I flee her office and head for my own, gathering my coat and bag before anyone can stop me. Alicia is coming out of Naia's office when I step out, and I offer her a tight smile before hurrying out the door.

3

CALEB

My alarm sounds from my phone, and I curse, knowing I have to do this or things will only get worse. I've been skipping my physical therapy exercises between sessions, and my doctor scolded me last time. Now there's a daily alarm on my phone so I won't forget. I pull out the instruction sheet he sent me home with and study the exercises. Each one is outlined in precise order and paired with horrible instructional diagrams.

For the next half hour, I work through each step, writing what I've done so I can take a picture and send it to my physical therapist as proof of my compliance. He told me that as long as I checked in every day, I wouldn't have to come in as much.

I hate that I have to take it easy. Even the simplest exercises make the muscles in my back spasm. The doctors assured me I was on pace to heal fully as long as I stuck to the routine. It's been almost three years now, and it still rankles that I'm not back to the old me.

Sherman watches, probably waiting for me to fall on my

ass. When I finish, he rotates in his cat tree to face the window. He likes to watch the birds in the winter since they're easier to spot at the feeder without all the leaves in the way.

I leave him to his business and tromp out.

Other than the parts I need for the heater that are supposed to arrive today, I don't know why I even bother going to the mailbox anymore. The only things in there are bills and junk mail. I can easily get rid of the junk mail in my fireplace; the bills, not so much. Even if I burned away the paper statements, the balances would still be there.

This winter has been tough, and we're not even halfway through. Between some unseasonably cool weather, extra snow, and the mounting repairs that the freezing temps have revealed, I'm shelling out money every day. If this keeps up like it would in a normal year, the freezing temperatures could last well into the spring.

The money I set aside for marketing is the only thing saving me from having to take out a second mortgage on the property. But that also means I haven't been advertising. The early-season bookings I was counting on to beef up my bank account in the spring aren't there since no one knows about us outside of the area.

This means that there'll be fewer reviews and less of a chance for reservations during the peak of tourist season. My previous foolproof business plan is falling apart by the day, just like the property.

Between water pipes bursting multiple times, spotty insulation in some of the exterior walls, and a failed heater in the lighthouse, I've become good friends with the local hardware store owner.

Thank god he gives me a discount.

I had a few winter bookings but had to cancel half of them because of the repairs, so I wound up losing money there, too. *You need to think about something else,* I counsel myself. If I dwell on this much longer, I won't stop spiraling, and that's never done me any good.

The walk down my long driveway wakes me up, crisp air stealing my breath as it swoops in from the lake. Birds call to one another from the trees and waves crash against the cliff walls, but other than that, there's no other sound. It's part of the reason I bought this property, even though it had more fixing up than I originally planned for.

I find the packages I need inside my oversized box. Amazing how something so small can wreck an entire furnace's ability to function. My tools are still laid out in the lighthouse since I partially disassembled the thing to figure out what went wrong and didn't see the need to put it all back together before the parts arrived.

There are a few pieces of junk mail that I stuff in my pocket before turning my face up to the sky. For once, it's clear and blue, the sun shining down without a cloud in sight. It awes me how much of a difference a sunny day makes in how I'm feeling. Especially now, with so much pressure building around my business.

After everything that happened while I was in the Army and then getting discharged, I can't seem to get out of my head. The doctors gave it a few labels, but I know winter makes it harder, the dark days and cold making me stiffen up and think about everything and what my life would have been like if I were still enlisted.

The lighthouse stands tall and white against the sky as I head for the visitor's door. If I hurry, I might be able to get a jump start on repairs before it gets too cold.

Several hours later, I look up and swipe at the sweat dotting my forehead. “What are you two doing here?” I rub at my neck where the longer hairs are starting to get irritating. A haircut is also on my to-do list, but it’s low priority.

“You weren’t answering your phone,” Matt says. Steve finishes with, “Again.”

Matt gives him a look and then turns back to me. “We were concerned. I know you didn’t have any bookings the last few weeks.”

“We wanted to make sure you weren’t torturing yourself with any more solitary confinement,” Steve adds.

“Do those confined have to fix heaters regularly?” I raise an eyebrow in question. “Because if so, then I guess that’s me.”

“Can’t say it feels like it’s fixed yet.” Matt smirks.

“You going to help?” I hold a wrench out to him, and to my surprise, he takes it, leaning into the open side of the heater and looking around. “Do you actually know what you’re doing?”

“More than you. Give me a minute.” Matt takes off his jacket and rolls up his sleeves.

Steve and I both offer unhelpful suggestions while Matt does the job to get the stupid thing back working. It comes to life with a low hum and a blessed blast of heat.

“Should be good now. You would’ve gotten there sooner or later.” Matt looks over his shoulder with a shit-eating grin, and I resist the urge to hit him. Not hard, but just enough so he knows I don’t think he’s as funny as he thinks he is.

"C'mon. It won't do us any good to stand in the cold. Let's go back to your cabin." Steve tosses Matt his coat.

I look back and forth between the two of them. "Why?"

"Well, he probably wants a beer, and I want to visit with Sherman." Matt pulls his coat on and tugs out a stocking cap from the pocket.

"I could use a beer." Steve nods and pulls the door open, letting in a blast of even colder air.

I lead them across the snow-covered lawn and the narrow trail that leads to my cabin. The roofline is more visible in winter without the foliage walling it off, but it's solidly separated from the rest of the property in the summer, giving me what I hope will be a modicum of privacy.

Sherman, traitor that he is, leaps down from his cat tree and coos all the way over to Matt when he comes in. Kicking off my boots and hanging my coat gives me a few moments to figure out why these two showed up out of the blue in the middle of the afternoon on a Wednesday.

They're used to me not answering my phone, so it can't just be that. *Dammit, Matt's still down as my emergency contact.* Sighing, I make my way to the fridge and pull out two beers and a bottle of water. I'm assuming Matt's driving, plus he's not much of a drinker anyway.

"Thanks." They both fall into armchairs, so I sprawl on the couch. As soon as Matt sits, Sherman leaps into his lap.

We all stare at each other for a minute before Steve reaches for the remote and turns on the TV. He flips through until he reaches a sports channel, lowers the volume, and then polishes off the beer while all of us sit there in silence. "There. Now, at least there's some noise."

I can't help the snort that escapes me. Steve never could

stand to linger in silence. He would hate living out here. Me, I thrive on it. It gives me a lot of time with my thoughts, which might not be the best idea, but at least I don't have to inflict my piss-poor attitude on other people if I don't want to.

The solitude also gives me something to focus on. Every day, there's something to work on, so I know I have to get up and move because there's no one else to rely on. In some ways, it's cathartic. Working with my hands has always been something that helps me think, and I enjoy learning new things.

"Best not beat around the bush." I look pointedly at Matt.

"Your doctor called. Said you've missed a couple of appointments." Matt sets the bottle of water aside so he can use both hands to scratch Sherman's chin. "They were worried. And since we didn't know you were still supposed to be going that often, we were worried too."

I'd let them think it was only a minor injury and that I just chose not to reenlist afterward. "It's fine. I've got it under control." And I do. I'm feeling better already. Or at least that's what I keep telling myself.

Matt looks skeptical. "He mentioned I should pass on some info about a support group, too."

My eyes roll, a front to mask my disgruntlement. Dr. Black keeps suggesting I go to the outreach group hosted at the VA, but I don't want to. So many other people have been affected so much more than me. I should be able to deal with these things on my own, and I don't want to minimize what other people have been through. "Thanks."

We all watch the scrolling news ticker for a moment before Steve slaps his knee. "Alright, tell us how you're really doing." When I protest, he holds a hand up. "Not that stuff, unless you actually talk about it. I meant business stuff. I know how hard this time of year is, and you already said you've had to cancel a few reservations. Just be honest with us."

This was much safer territory. "It's going. How about you guys?"

"It's been slow, but that's expected. We've been putting a lot of work into getting ready for the growing season in the greenhouse, and Harry stopped by again last week, which kept us on our toes." Steve grins at the mention of his and Andrea's business partner.

"And I'm steady as usual. God bless the snowfall this month. It keeps me working almost every week."

"Wish you were closer," I mutter against the lip of my bottle. I've been using the four-wheeler to clear smaller paths, but I'll have to attach the plow to the front of the truck sometime soon.

"Us too." Matt sounds sincere. We've been tight since childhood and still are, but the distance and our busy lives make it harder to get together as much as we used to.

"While we're here, Andrea wanted me to remind you to confirm the dates you wanted to do those special dinners. She was hoping to block them out before the summer gets booked out."

Those would at least give me something on the calendar, which also meant I could advertise. Andrea and I had talked about hosting an event every other month at the B and B to highlight both of our businesses. "I'll email her by the end of the week. And Matt, let Lenore know the ads seem to work. A few people booked last week, so now July is almost full, and August is about three-quarters of the way there."

She was running ads on my shoestring budget and letting me keep a tab if I couldn't pay that month.

"Good to hear." He smiles and helps Sherman to the floor before he stands up and stretches.

"Now that we've got all that out of the way and we're here, we can either sit around and gripe or get something done." Steve smacks his hands against his knees and stands, too. "Where's your to-do list?"

THE GUYS DON'T LEAVE until well after dark, and when they do, I'm more energized than I have been in weeks.

While I try to unwind, I putter around the cabin, cleaning and putting away a load of laundry. When the first yawn hits, I capitalize on the approaching tiredness and crawl into bed. For once, sleep creeps up quickly as I nod off. My last thoughts before passing out were of how nice it was to have people around. Nice, but also exhausting because all day, I had to pretend everything was okay.

4

MONICA

I feel like I've cataloged every mark and crack on the walls and ceiling of my apartment. It's only been a week since I've been on sabbatical, but I feel like I'm going crazy. Even if I have nothing to do, I force myself to go outside at least once a day so I don't turn into a completely paranoid mess.

Needless to say, I don't do well without work, and my life has revolved around exactly that for years. I don't have any hobbies, and all my friends are working. I never had time to work on any healthy habits like going to the gym or volunteering.

If my career had gone off the rails like this last year, I would call Alana, who'd sneak me information so I could at least keep working. But I don't even have that anymore.

Well, I could still call her, but nothing good would come from that. If anyone found out, my testimony would be called into question. Plus, she's under house arrest, and I don't even know what I would say to her. She tried to reach out a few times, but I haven't responded.

I could call Sarah. She works from home, so she wouldn't get in trouble for having personal conversations during work. Maybe she'll even let me come up there and visit. Or lay on her couch and stare at her ceiling instead of my own.

Are you very busy today?

I send the message before I can overthink it.

Not really. Things will pick up next month once taxes start rolling in for the end of the year.

There's a brief pause before another message comes through.

What about you? You've got to be swamped with everything going on.

A wry smile pulls at my lips, and I debate how to make this sound less pitiful than it is.

I'm actually on a bit of a break at the moment.

Without wanting to see how she responds, I flip my phone face down on the table. In a rush, I stand and pace back and forth across the living room. I need to do laundry one of these days, noticing the pile in the corner and scowling.

Not today.

I stalk back over to the table and flip over my phone to read Sarah's response.

You? Taking a break?

I don't want to lie to my friend, so I fess up.

It wasn't my idea, and it's only for a little while.

My phone rings before I set it down.

"What's going on? What do you need? How can we help?" All the sentences run together in a rush.

"My bosses asked me to take a sabbatical." I switch the phone to speaker and set it on the table before throwing myself back on the couch. "They're concerned about my well-being."

"Well. . ." Sarah trails off.

"What?"

"You have been burning the candle at both ends. I've seen the time you take to respond to group texts and emails."

I can't argue with that, so I just stay quiet.

"When did this happen?" Sarah asks, concern tingeing her words.

"Last week." My voice is weak, even to my ears.

"How soon can you get here?"

"So you've been wallowing at home for a week without reaching out to us?" Andrea glares at me while Sarah and Nore sit beside her. They look at me with the exact expression of sympathy I was trying to avoid.

"More or less." There's no explaining the way my brain works. Between my run-in with Caleb on Halloween and everything that happened in the spring, I've been doubting myself and the people around me. I'd rather become one with my couch than reach out for help or attempt to connect with people.

"Why?" Andrea still looks irritated.

"Ah..."

"We're your friends. That's what we're here for." Sarah's voice is soft, but I still feel like I'm being chastised.

"I'm sorry?" I sip at the glass of wine Sarah has kept refilled for the last couple of hours.

Ever the peacemaker, Nore comes over and sits next to

me. She wraps her arms around my shoulders and squeezes me close. "We're always here for you when you need us, hon."

Tears well in my eyes, and I try to sniff them back. "Thanks."

"Don't tell Steve I made you cry. He'll yell at me for being too pushy again." Andrea tries to lighten the mood.

"What are you going to do in the meantime? I'm assuming they're not letting you go back soon?" Sarah asks, leaning back into the corner of the couch.

"I don't know, but I'm going nuts staying at home all day. Since it's winter, it's not like I can go on a lot of walks or do things outside."

Despair, helplessness, and frustration are all unfamiliar emotions, and I'm not equipped to deal with them. Usually, I bury everything and try to ignore it until it goes away, but when you're faced with eighteen hours of free time a day and you have trouble sleeping, it gets hard to keep up the charade.

"You should take a vacation." Andrea chomps through the crackers Sarah set out earlier.

"They are paying me while I'm on sabbatical..." I like the idea of a vacation, but again, it's the middle of winter, and every place worth going to will be a million miles away. With Christmas next week, last-minute flights are going to be astronomically expensive.

But I could go after the new year, two weeks from now.

"If you don't want to fly, you could do a staycation." Andrea looks like she wouldn't mind one, too. "There are plenty of open rental properties around here, and I'm sure the owners would appreciate the business in the off-season."

Nore straightens up suddenly. "You should call Caleb

and see if you can rent the bed-and-breakfast. It's close-ish, so it's not too far away. The view is beautiful, and it's peaceful enough that you might get to relax but still be near enough that we could come visit you."

"No." The word is vehement.

"Why not?" Nore looks affronted.

How do I explain this to them without being offensive? I know they all like and get along with Caleb, but that isn't the case for me. We put up a good front when everyone saw us together in the spring, but we've been studiously avoiding each other ever since. "We don't get along."

"How can you not get along with Caleb?" Andrea looks genuinely confused. "He's great. Doesn't talk too much, always willing to help out when he can."

Sarah, who's watching me with narrowed eyes, seems to be the only one who understands that the situation is more complicated than I'm letting on. For a quiet woman, she's scarily observant when she wants to be.

"We just don't. Nothing against him." Everything against him. "Our personalities don't mesh."

"Did something happen?" Nore is always willing to dive in and solve everyone's problems if we let her.

I'd rather not talk about this with them. "We just don't see eye to eye on anything." Well, we saw eye to eye on something, briefly, before everything went to shit.

"Did you scare him?" Andrea asks with a hint of sarcasm.

"How would *I* scare *him*?" *Was that even possible?*

"You have a... um, strong... personality. Especially when faced with a challenge." Sarah tries to smooth things over.

"And that man is a delicious challenge," Andrea mutters.

Nore and Sarah both stare at her, mouths open in shock, and I snort into the wine glass I'm using to hide my face.

"What? You can't deny he's hot. Plus, he's got this whole broody loner thing going on." Andrea grins and waggles her eyebrows.

Sarah laughs but tries to play it off as a cough.

"See!" Andrea points at her. "You know what I'm talking about. Just because I'm not single anymore doesn't mean I've gone blind." We burst out in a fit of giggles that turns into uncontrollable laughter whenever we try to make eye contact with each other.

When my sides feel like they're caving in, I take gasping breaths of air to calm down. Nore's still shaking with silent laughter next to me, curled into a ball with a pillow shoved against her face.

"Why do I feel like you're trying to set us up?" I mock glare at Andrea, who has the audacity to shrug. "Oh my god, you are!"

"I think you'd be cute together." Andrea looks hopeful.

"Look, just because you three have happy, stable, romantic relationships doesn't mean I need one."

They all give me the same pitying look.

"I don't!"

"Maybe not right now, but just keep an open mind about the future," Nore says, patting my knee. "But seriously. I think you should stay at Caleb's for a little while. It's private, at the very least, so you could get away from your dad."

That would be an enormous benefit. "I'll think about it."

"That's all I ask." Andrea takes a swig of her drink. "The boys should be here soon. You staying with Sarah or hitching a ride home with me and Steve?"

The idea of having a sleepover at Sarah's has appeal, but I didn't bring anything with me. "Ride, please."

"Bret and I will bring the car down tomorrow." Sarah smiles and stands, collecting the now-empty wine bottle and heading for the kitchen. "Anyone want some more snacks?"

We all cheer, and she laughs, raiding her treat cupboard to get us the good stuff.

THEY'RE GOING to ask if I called him. If I lie, they'll probably catch me since someone will ask him. Then he'll have even more ammunition to launch at me. Not that I know why we're at odds, other than that he enjoys irritating me ever since the hospital in the spring. Thankfully, neither of us was seriously injured after the car accident, but he had to hold something against me.

I'm going to have to call him. There's no way to avoid it now.

I've managed to stall for a few days to try to rationalize this insane idea. The one thing that convinced me was that I could literally escape my father and his insane persistence that I follow his idealized career goals for me.

My thumb hovers over Caleb's contact info, and I fight the urge to clear it. Before I realize what's happening, the call is going through and Caleb answers after only one ring. In a fumble, I almost drop the phone and swear.

"Hello?" His deep voice sounds questioning but not concerned.

"Sorry. Almost dropped the phone," I blurt out.

"Did you mean to call me?" Now he sounds straight-up

confused. It stings my ego. After hooking up with someone, you usually still want them to speak to you civilly, even if the aftermath has resulted in tension. We still have mutual friends, so it isn't unheard of that I might call him from time to time. You know, to relay information or something.

"Yes," I say. The silence has dragged on just a touch too long to make the statement believable.

He sighs. The sound carries the same exhaustion that I feel every moment of every day. "Why? I have other things I could be doing other than listening to you breathe on the phone."

There's the asshole I know. "You know, I've never heard you treat anyone else this way. Would it kill you to be civil for one phone call?"

"Based on this conversation, yes."

If he were here, I'd probably get that self-satisfied smirk. There's a hint of it in his voice, and my blood boils. "You're such a prick, you know that?"

"Yeah." He's not at all ashamed about it, either.

I grit my teeth, trying to think of a way to get this conversation back on track.

"Time's a ticking, princess."

I growl. "Stop calling me that."

"But it suits you so well." I'm sure he's grinning now and full of self-satisfaction because it's so easy for him to get under my skin. To my utter shame, no quick responses come to mind, and more awkward silence fills the line. "My god, have I made you speechless?" He's outright laughing now, and I would strangle him if he was here.

"No. I'm counting backward from a hundred so I won't say something I'll regret later."

His laughter is enticing. Deep and rusty, like he doesn't

do it very often. "Why don't you just tell me why you called?"

At this exact moment, I would rather do anything else than ask him for something, but I've backed myself into a corner, and now I have to. "I need a favor."

Thankfully, he doesn't laugh. He makes a contemplative sound and waits.

"I was wondering if it might be possible to arrange a longer-term reservation for the bed-and-breakfast. Maybe a few weeks, but leave it open-ended? You know, in case the person would like to stay longer. And private. It'd be for the entire house." The small, hopeful part of my brain that's still active wants him to say no, he can't do it.

"For winter?" He sounds shocked.

"Yeah. For January and maybe into February?" If I make it sound longer, maybe there's a chance he'll say no. He has to have some reservations booked somewhere during that time, right? And it would be bad for business to cancel reservations.

"They know I don't cook, right? If they need me to, I'm willing to help with grocery runs, but there's no pre-made food," he says almost cheerfully, and I wonder if I've made this too appealing. Maybe he didn't have any reservations, and the prospect of being paid for two months is a can't-miss opportunity. Shit, now I feel slightly bad. It's his first year of business. He probably needs the money.

"They know."

"Do you know what they plan on doing? I could recommend some outdoor spots. Maybe put together a list of places that are still open during the winter and send it over with all of the info they'll need."

I should let him do all that work. It'd be a fun way to keep up this ruse. "They would love that, thank you."

He's sounding excited, and it's amazing how much more personable he is when we're not picking at each other. "I'll email you all the details, and you can send me specifics as you get them."

"Will do. The New Year's arrival date is firm, so we can start there."

"Thank you, Monica. You don't know how much I appreciate this." He's grateful. The realization shocks me into silence. It almost makes me feel bad for not telling him this is for me. That we'll be stuck by each other for an extended time.

But I need this.

My father called again this morning, bugging me about making a decision between moving to an ADA position or taking over my brother's vacated state senate seat. His options still don't look any more appealing despite the time and space I've put between us.

"Thank you for being open to it," I mumble. Not wanting to push the civil interaction we're having beyond its natural limits, I wrap up the call and hang up.

I stare at the blank spot on the wall for a minute, processing, before the urge to move, to do something, comes over me, and I stand, pacing across the floor with no particular goal in mind.

The energy that's been missing for what feels like months now is back, but I refuse to associate that with my conversation with Caleb. It's definitely just because I have a plan now and a potential break from my father.

I just have to get through Christmas and make it to New Year's.

5

CALEB

Matt and Nore convinced me to come to their house for Christmas. Apparently, "everyone was coming over," and that alone almost made me want to say no. After that phone call and a series of snarky emails exchanged with Monica over the last week, I still wasn't ready to see her in person.

The confounding woman. I was so surprised when she called and asked for an extended reservation that I tried to put the things I've been working on with my therapist into practice. But I don't necessarily trust the strength of that practice in person and don't want to ruin everyone else's holiday by fighting with her.

Before I could tell him no, Steve casually let it slip that Monica was going to her grandma's, so it would be Price-free if I came. It pisses me off that I'm letting my feelings for her show enough that Steve can pick up on them, but I agree to come down for a little while.

It was nice having all the old crew back together and getting a taste of Annie's cooking again. I went hunting with

Al in November, but deer camp food is nowhere near as good as Annie's holiday menu.

I rush through my PT exercises, and Sherman gives me a knowing look. This extended-stay situation is making me nervous. All the things that can go wrong circle through my mind. After having the prospect of two months of unexpected payments dangled in front of me, I can't afford to screw this up.

It could be the difference between me staying in business or going bust by the end of the summer. Not only would it pay off my tab with Lenore and fund more advertising, but getting paid for two months could bring down my credit card bills and give me a jump start on loan repayments for this year.

The person who booked the house is supposed to get here around noon, and I want to do a last walk-through to make sure everything is set up. And that nothing else has broken overnight.

So far, the pipes and heater have both held through the last few weeks of freezing weather. I cross my fingers and toes and hope that the wind takes it easy and doesn't rip off any more shutters. A niggle of suspicion tickles my brain, but I tamp it down. If this were a regular stay, I would have put the guest's name on the welcome board, but Monica has been cagey about giving me details.

With one last paranoid examination, I try to wrangle my incessant worry about something going wrong. A car pulls up outside, and my heart rate speeds up. I shake out my hands a few times, trying to do some of the breathing techniques that the therapists have recommended to help me stay focused.

They're early. It can't be anyone else. No one else comes

out here unless they're checking in. Or they're my friends doing a welfare check.

Steeling myself to greet the stranger, I push open the front door and freeze in my tracks. It's Monica's gray Lexus, a newer version of the same model she crashed last spring. It's parked in the lot, and I can see Monica's long, glimmering black hair through the driver's side window.

My gut does a confused swoop, unsure if I should be excited, irritated, or nonchalant about her arrival. Even before she called for the reservation, she'd been on my mind more often than I'll admit. And now she's here.

Maybe she's just dropping her friend off? My luck couldn't be that good.

I squint, trying to see if anyone else is in the car, but all I can make out is a mass of suitcases in the backseat.

When her foot touches the ground, the first thing I notice is the lack of her trusty three-inch heels. Instead, she's wearing practical winter boots. They look brand new, but at least she won't kill herself walking in the snow. I do my best to keep the sidewalks clear and salted, but we're still right on the lake.

My eyes trail up her jean-clad leg, another surprise since I've only seen her in business wear, and come to a grinding halt on her perfectly round and toned ass. She's bending down to pull something out from the driver's seat, and it's just... there.

Attraction tries to pique my interest, but I fight it down. *We tried that road before, and it didn't end well,* I remind myself.

She straightens, slinging a large briefcase and purse over her shoulder before she turns to face me, halting when she realizes I've been watching her.

Her long, elegant fingers brush non-existent hair off her face in a nervous gesture. Something about it staves off my irritation. She's just as uncertain about this as I am, and she must have had a good reason for not telling me it was her coming. *Could something have happened? Is this supposed to be some sort of hideout for her? Could something else have come up about the case?*

No, she would have said something if the criminal organization Alana was working with was after her again because it would mean I'd be in danger. Plus, Steve and Andrea would be too. As much as she hates me now, she wouldn't risk her friends' safety by keeping them out of the loop.

Curiosity overrules all my other roiling emotions, and I hold my place by the door, waiting for her to come to me. It's rare that I don't see her confident, and the vulnerability coming through is drawing me in.

She squares her shoulders and lifts her chin, approaching with measured steps. Since I suspect she's my extended guest, I hold out a hand for her bags when she gets within arm's reach. *Good service equals good reviews,* I repeat over and over.

Except she looks at me like I'm trying to rob her and doesn't hand over anything. "I can take your bags for you." I look at the shoulder being weighed down with the briefcase.

"That's alright." Her nose scrunches in what, even I admit, is an adorable wrinkle.

"O... kay." I step aside and push the door open. "Why don't you come in out of the cold? Wind's a little harsh today." She looks at the gap between me and the door frame before stepping past, taking care not to brush against me or hit me with the bulging briefcase.

She acts like I have a contagious disease, and it reminds me why we're in this situation. I scowl, letting the door bang shut behind me. She jumps and spins around, noting the return of my normal, non-customer service face.

It seems to make her relax.

"I'm assuming you're the friend who needed a place to stay for a while?" I motion toward the reception area, and she follows me.

"Yes. About that..." She trails off, looking around with curiosity. "This place is really nice. The girls said you did most of the work yourself?"

I fight a smile at her blatant redirect. "I did. You want to pick your room? There are three upstairs and one down here."

"Downstairs is fine."

She says it so quickly I'm taken aback. I was expecting her to want to check out each room and pick apart any detail that wasn't up to her standards. "You don't even want to see it first?"

"No, I'm sure it's good." She sets her bag on the chair and tries to be subtle about rolling the stress out of her shoulders. I raise an eyebrow but don't contradict her. "What? Are you saying one of your rooms is inferior?" Pink rises in her cheeks, and she looks less defeated than she did when she first got out of the car.

"Maybe I'm just trying to accommodate a guest with refined taste."

Her lips purse and her cheeks darken more, but she doesn't take the bait. "What information do you need to check me in?"

I rotate the monitor so she can type in her info, and I

step out from behind the desk. "While you're filling that out, I can get your bags. You're sure about the downstairs room?"

"I can get my bags." Her words come out in a rush. "There are confidential files." She trails off.

Like I'd spy on her. "It's not a big deal." She huffs in annoyance at my continued persistence. "All part of the service, and I promise not to look." I turn and walk toward the car before she can argue. The sound of her growl of frustration follows me, and I chuckle, feeling more alive than I have in the last few months.

SHERMAN and I lounge on the couch, attempting to watch a movie. What's really happening is me staring out the window toward the guest house, where three windows are still lit up.

I never pegged her as a night owl, but it looks like we have something in common. The few days I stayed with her this spring, she mostly locked herself in her room and didn't make a sound. I assumed it was her sleeping.

Looks like I was wrong.

I turn the TV off and sit in the dark. Sherman stretches and turns against my side, hiding his head under his fluffy tail and resuming his snoring. Why does a part of me want to go over there and check if she's alright?

It's stupid. Of course, she's alright.

I saw the amount of work she schlepped inside. Three cardboard boxes filled with files and two duffle bags of clothes and "necessities," as she'd labeled them. She was just working late, doing things she didn't need to be doing.

Nore told me that Monica was on a sabbatical from her

law firm and was supposed to be taking a break. I called her when I got back to the house earlier to pump her for information.

But she's annoyingly loyal to Monica and didn't let much slip. Maybe I could get more information directly from the source tomorrow. Part of my bed-and-breakfast services are daily cleanings and turn-downs, so I'll have to go over there at some point.

I'm not tired, so there's no use trying to sleep. There's a handful of larger branches I've been meaning to cut up for firewood, and the backyard flood light will keep everything illuminated. It shouldn't bother Monica. Between my cabin and the trees, most of the light will be blocked, and it's not like she'll be looking this way anyway. I didn't tell her my cabin was so close.

Sherman grumbles when I stand up but doesn't open his eyes. I put my boots on and grab a bottle of water before heading outside to get to work.

In the morning, I fight the urge to go over to the guest house right away. If she was up late, the odds of her being awake early are slim, and I don't want to barge in on her. Despite our antagonism, she is a guest now and is paying to be here. I owe her at least that much respect.

I dump Sherman's food into his bowl and fry up some bacon and eggs. I don't eat much, but I have a mild coffee addiction, so I make a full pot that will keep me going for the day ahead. Since Monica's here, I can't work on things up at the house like I have been. Seems like it's time to tackle the paperwork I've been putting off.

After I finish breakfast and clean up, I head to the small second bedroom that I converted into an office when I moved in.

With a groan, I settle my butt on the seat of the cheap office chair and open my accounting program on the computer. Might as well get the worst thing out of the way first. To my surprise, I enjoy the marketing aspects of running a business, and with Nore's help, our efforts have been doing better than if I tried on my own.

The numbers are swimming in front of my eyes when an email notification pops up. Needing a break from accounting, I switch over and see an email from Monica. Why didn't she just text me if she needed something?

I open the message and find a brief note asking me to sign the attached NDA.

Why the hell would she need me to sign an NDA?

Opening it up, I try to read through it, but it's full of legalese, and there's no explanation about what the hell is going on. I print it out to see if reading it on paper will help. It doesn't.

Infuriated, I shove my chair back and storm out of the office, papers clutched in my hand. I shove my feet into boots, not bothering to lace them up, and slam out of the door. My long strides close the distance between my cabin and the guest house in no time. Forgoing a knock on the door, I storm in and am greeted with a squeak from the couch.

"What the fuck is this?"

She scrambles up from where she's surrounded by files. Once she's on her feet, she stands tall but pulls her cardigan tighter around her slim frame.

"How the hell would I know?" She glares despite still being visibly surprised by my unannounced entrance.

"You sent it to me." I brandish the papers at her like a bullfighter's cape.

"Oh." She calms down almost instantly. "It's a nondisclosure agreement. You could have signed electronically. No need to waste paper." I raise an eyebrow and take in the mountains of paper she's moved into my space. "I know it's a little ironic."

Why isn't she getting irritated? To my horror, I realize I'm hoping for a fight or at least a rousing disagreement. Arguing with her is easier than untangling all of my emotions.

Monica Price is annoying, entitled, and intelligent. She's a challenge I shouldn't want to unravel. I double down on my hostility. "Let me put this in simpler terms. Why do I need to sign an NDA? Is there something going on with the case I should know about?"

Her face pales, and she takes a step toward me, arm outstretched. "Oh god, no, I'm sorry. I should have known you'd assume that."

But she doesn't say anything else. I'm used to being in somewhat of a position of authority and having people give me the answers that I want when I want them. Monica doesn't give two shits about doing what I want. "Then please explain to me what the fuck you need me to sign these for."

Her cheeks color, and in that moment, she looks like a modern-day Snow White. Rosy cheeks, raven black hair, pale skin. Too pale. I study her more closely, looking for signs that something else is wrong. Maybe she's sick, and that's why she had to take a break.

"You know, my grandma always said that swearing is a

sign of an uncreative mind." She smirks, thinking she has the upper hand.

"I prefer the argument that fuck is one of the most versatile words in the English language." I smirk back, letting the insinuation lace my words. If she doesn't understand the implication, the slow sweep of my gaze down her body should make it obvious.

"If I tell you why I need you to sign the NDA, will you promise to go away and knock before you come in from now on?" If possible, her cheeks are even redder than they were before.

"Possibly." I take a step closer to her, and she stares at my feet.

"Why didn't you lace up your shoes? And how did you get here so fast? I only sent that fifteen minutes ago." Her eyes track back upward. "And you don't have a coat on. It's got to be fifteen degrees outside at most."

"You're not my mom. Don't worry about me," I snark on instinct, but her concern about my well-being warms something long dormant in my chest.

"Is it impossible for you *not* to be an ass, even with your guests?" she snaps, and I relax.

"Can you just be honest with me and tell me why I need to sign an NDA?"

"Fine. I don't want my dad to know I'm here. If it wasn't clear before, I don't want anyone to know I'm here because it might get back to him."

So the princess is annoyed with Daddy Dearest. "Please elaborate."

Her arms cross, and her hip pops out to the side. "I don't want to."

"Why?" I mirror her pose.

"Because you'll use it against me."

I study her defensive posture and the way her shoulders are creeping closer to her ears. She looks more vulnerable as she tries to shield herself. "I promise I won't."

She studies me like she'd be able to tell if I was lying. Although part of me still wants her to trust me. A stupid, foolish part. "They asked me to take a leave of absence. On top of everything else going on, my father can't find out. If he does, I'll never be able to make a career decision on my own again."

Obviously, I know who her father is. Everyone in the area does. I also know how close she is with him and how alike they seem on the surface. Is it possible there's a rift in the Price family's perfect facade?

"So you're hiding out from your father? What if he goes to your office? What are they going to tell him?"

She shifts her feet and looks away. "I asked them to sign NDAs too."

That makes me feel less offended. "At least I'm not the only one. What about your friends? Did you make them sign one, too?" I can't decide if I want her to say yes or no.

"No!" She glares. "I trust them, and this was their idea, anyway. When Nore saw how stir-crazy I was going in my apartment, she suggested I call you."

"You're willing to take that risk?" *Keep prodding. Make her angry. Start a fight. It's the only time you feel alive anymore.* My therapist is going to have a field day with this when he finds out.

"They're my friends." She sounds almost childlike in her defense, blindly trusting them to keep her secret.

"So I guess I'm not your friend, then?" I don't know why I say it or how I'm hoping she'll respond. Her jaw drops in shock, and she looks stunned that I'd even ask. "I'll sign your stupid contract. Where's a pen?"

Before she can hand me one, I spot the cup full of them on the check-in desk and stride over to it, signing my name in an angry slash and leaving the paperwork on the desktop.

Without saying another word, I walk out, letting the door close behind me. Guilt follows me all the way back to the cabin, but I'm definitely not fleeing.

I SLEEP like shit that night and wake up before the sun, pacing around the cabin and getting glared at by Sherman. Everything that happened yesterday plays on an unending loop in my head. The look of hurt on Monica's face. How much of an ass I'd been. The complete abandonment of all the skills and coping mechanisms I've been working on in therapy.

The need to apologize chases me hard, dogging my heels and consuming my motivation to do anything else.

Stalling to avoid the inevitable apology that I'll make, I text my therapist to see if he has any appointments available today. It's been a while since I've talked to him, so I have a feeling even if he doesn't, he'll make room.

Sure enough, I get a message within the hour that he has some space before lunchtime. Confirming the appointment, I get dressed and make coffee before settling on the couch, where I can see just a sliver of the guest house.

6

MONICA

I've been here for two weeks so far, and other than the run-in with Caleb the morning after I arrived and his reluctant apology the next day, I haven't seen him.

He's like a wraith. I know he lives close by, so I've been peeking out the windows, trying to see where he's coming from, but I still haven't caught him. Other than snooping for signs of Caleb and burying myself in the files that I brought with me, I haven't done much, which makes me antsy.

He has to be getting in here somehow, though. The rooms stay clean, the sheets get washed, and food appears from the grocery store like magic. But I never see him. It makes me think that he's not only avoiding me but also watching to see when h' can sneak over and get his work done. Which creeps me out less than it should.

Caleb has become a conundrum that I can't figure out. Instead of fighting with me like I expected him to, he's freezing me out. I'm not sure how I feel about it other than it making me more curious about him. He can be such an ass, but then he does these little things that make me think he cares.

Like with the grocery deliveries. He clearly noticed what I was eating and not eating. One morning, I got an email asking me what brands I prefer. Plus, when he realized I mostly eat trash food, he started slipping in healthier options that are shockingly good. In one very surreal text last week, he suggested I pick out a few recipes that I want to try to make, and he'll get all the ingredients. Could this be his way of encouraging me to do something other than work?

He never once asked about the cost or sent me a bill. I assumed he would put it on the final invoice, but we never talked about it. We never talk about anything.

The walk to the lighthouse should help me clear my head.

Even though the path between the guest house and the lighthouse is short, I like to go up and down the spiral stairs a few times and look out at the lake, which takes at least a half hour. After the first couple of days, I realized the weather here changes much faster than I'm used to.

On one of my daily hikes, I got to the top just as a winter storm was rolling in. The wind was fierce, almost so strong I thought it'd pop the window out of its frame. Despite the worry, the sheer power of it enthralled me. I stood rooted to the spot in the middle of the upper floor, watching the clouds and wind and the blowing snow and rain.

The only thing that brought me out of the trance was a buzzing from my phone with a terse message from Caleb asking if I needed a ride back to the house. I told him no, waiting for the worst of the storm to pass and then dashing through the murky daylight until I made it safely inside.

Today's forecast calls for plummeting temperatures and a potential ice storm. Deciding to err on the side of caution, I opt for staying here and climbing up and down the much less scenic staircase in the guest house. After that first storm, Caleb dropped some stern warnings about watching for ice buildup and mentioned how the door froze shut for almost a week last month.

If I didn't know better, I'd say he's worried about me.

After I do a few laps, I'm focused enough to try tackling some work again. Contracts are honestly one of my favorite parts of practicing law, so I bargained to work on those while I was out of the office. The flashier parts of the law—the public court cases, arguing in front of a jury, and making bold statements to the press—were always what my dad preferred. I tend to gravitate toward the more academic elements.

A few hours pass in the blink of an eye when I feel a drip hit my forehead. I wipe it away without thinking, but then a drip lands on my keyboard. The storm has been picking up in intensity. Could it have blown a window open upstairs?

I set aside my laptop and look up, trying to see where the drips are coming from. The ceiling is dark hardwood, and wherever the water is falling from blends in with the grain and low light.

The rooms upstairs are something I haven't explored, preferring to limit the areas Caleb has to clean as much as possible. I know we don't get along, but I still don't want to make his life harder for him. When it comes down to it, he's doing me a favor by letting me stay here. I'm sure he must have canceled at least a few reservations to make this happen.

Venturing beyond the staircase upstairs, I investigate

each room. Once again, I'm impressed with the work Caleb put in to get this place ready for guests. It's fully restored to make it modern but still has rustic touches. Local art graces the walls without being overwhelming, and the color scheme is warm and welcoming.

Taking a guess at where the problem might be, I turn right and start opening doors. I know there's no one else staying here, but it still feels like I'm intruding. Although the upstairs is much chillier than downstairs, the rooms still look cozy. Checking the first bathroom, I don't see any signs of water leaking, and the windows are all closed.

Moving on to the next room, I find a matching pair of twin beds and floral wallpaper on the walls. But once again, nothing looks wrong.

The last room is in the far corner of the second floor, on the southeast side, and directly above the living area and office.

The storm beats at the windows, but they're shut tightly. When I get to the bathroom, I slip on the slick tile, letting loose an inelegant grunt as I grab the sink to keep myself upright. Water covers the floor, and I groan, spying what looks like a burst pipe. Or at least one that's leaking enough to create a small pond.

This room is on the outer corner, so it's most exposed to the outdoor temperatures. With the arctic cold that came with this storm, the pipe couldn't keep up with the temps and froze over. It probably didn't help that no one was up here using it.

Shit.

I raid the linen cupboard for every available towel, but I already know it won't be enough. Dashing to the other rooms, I gather the piles of folded towels and hurry back in to layer them on the floor. Hopefully, they'll absorb the water before it freezes and turns into a skating rink.

While they soak up the water, I check all the rooms on the upper floor one more time to make sure nothing else is wet. Just to be safe, I turn the water on low. Then I go downstairs to find my computer and search for how you go about fixing a leaky pipe.

I didn't get a good look at where the leak was coming from, so I don't know if it's a connector or another part of the pipe. The one thing I know for sure is that I have to turn the heat on higher upstairs. Caleb might have turned it down when I told him I'd stay downstairs.

After I go to the upstairs thermostat and turn it up, I venture into the waterlogged bathroom. The towels have sopped up the worst of it, and I gather the heavy fabric and haul them downstairs. This is my mess for turning the stupid thing down in the first place. I won't foist washing and drying them on Caleb. Plus, if I put them back before he comes over, maybe he'll never find out anything was wrong.

After I remove the last towel and before I go scrounging for supplies in his basement, I try to get a closer look at the pipe in question.

With one of the few remaining dry towels, I wipe away the water and wait to see if more appears. I watch a drip bubble and slide down from where the bendy part of the pipe connects to the straight part. It might be what the video I watched called a screw joint, which should be an easy fix. I might not even have to turn the water off to fix it. If my luck holds, I'll only need a wrench that will fit around the pipe.

Time to head for the basement, I guess.

I don't know what size I'm looking for, so if I find a

wrench, I'm praying it either adjusts or there's a set with more than one size.

Like the upper floors, the basement is fastidiously clean and organized. A large toolbox is on the opposite side of the space, and I open its drawers until I find a row of wrenches neatly laid out from smallest to largest. I take a guess on three that look close. A roll of duct tape catches my eye, and I grab that, too. Duct tape is supposed to fix everything, right?

Hauling my new treasures upstairs, I cue up the video I found and watch it through two more times, pretending to do each step while I watch. My goal is to not make anything worse than what it was.

When I'm confident that I know at least the motions of what I should do, I approach the sink with small steps so I don't slip and crouch down, trying each wrench until I find one that fits around the joint.

Righty tighty, lefty loosey. I repeat to myself while I turn the wrench to the right. It doesn't feel like it moves very much, but maybe that's all it needs. I wipe the pipe clean and wait to see if any more water drips out.

To my utter relief, it doesn't.

Deciding to be brave, I ease the water knob on, waiting between each quarter turn to see if the leak comes back. Nothing happens, and I sigh, filled with pride that I've figured something house-related out.

The urge to call Grandma and brag about my accomplishments rides me hard, but then she'd know where I was and tell Mom, who'd let it slip to Dad, and my brief escape would be over.

Instead, I snap a selfie with a fully functioning pipe in the background.

I turn the water off and clean up the rest of the towels. Looks like I'll be doing a few loads of laundry this afternoon. Thanks to Caleb's decorating choices, the colors of the towels match each of the rooms, so I'll know where to return them.

The storm dies down after a few hours. I peek out the window and see the sheen of ice coating every available surface. The lighthouse glitters in the weak sun, and all the bare trees and bushes look like sparkling, frozen wands.

When I take the last load of towels upstairs, I get the urge to double-check and see if the pipe is still good. My confidence takes a plummeting dive when I open the door, and water once again covers the floor. This time, instead of just being a slow drip, a spurting spray of water is coming out of the joint in the pipe.

"Fuck," I groan. Maybe I should have added the duct tape, too. Or maybe I didn't get the tap turned off all the way. My last little bubble of hope vanishes when I turn the knob more firmly to the off position, and nothing changes. Other than I'm now soaked from the knees down from the spray.

I'm going to have to call Caleb.

Shit, shit, shit.

I pull up his number and hit call, waiting for a few rings before he answers. "Hello?"

"Hi. It's Monica. I think we might have a problem." Now out of spraying range, I watch the sink for a moment before grabbing the freshly laundered towels and layering them back on the floor once again.

"What's going on?" He sounds alert, and I'm relieved he's not being sarcastic.

"I think a pipe burst upstairs." I hate that I sound so unsure, but I'm just waiting for him to blame this on me.

"Shit. I'll be there in a minute. I don't suppose you know how to turn the water off?"

"No." That feels like something I should know how to do, but being an apartment dweller has left me without a lot of basic home care knowledge.

"I'll be there in a second." He hangs up, and I put my phone away, ready to cry in frustration. I want to think I'm at least capable of turning a bolt correctly to stop a leak. Trying to be a little more helpful, I go downstairs and retrieve the wrench that fit earlier, as well as the roll of duct tape.

Just in case.

By the time I get back upstairs, Caleb's bursting through the front door. One side of him is covered in snow, like he slipped and fell on the ice. I wince, knowing that it must have hurt, especially if he was moving quickly when he fell. Momentum is your enemy in winter when it comes to slipping on ice.

He takes in my wet pants and the wrench and duct tape in my hand. "Thanks." For once, he doesn't seem grumpy, just focused on the task at hand.

When he moves to go down the stairs, I see the stiffness in his gait. It's even more obvious on the side of his body where the snow is still sticking. "You okay?"

He freezes, rolling his shoulders, but doesn't turn around. "I'm fine. Don't worry."

He starts down the stairs, and I follow, wanting to see how to turn the water off.

"You don't have to follow me around," he snaps, but somehow the barbs don't seem as sharp as before. If the idiot's gone and gotten himself more seriously hurt than he's letting on, I don't want him to suffer. Some part of me still cares about him.

"I want to see how to turn the water off."

"Why?" He glances at me but keeps moving.

"Because I don't know how." It's an explanation that makes perfect sense to me but seems to befuddle him.

He finds a small wheel on a pipe that leads into the ceiling and turns it to the right until it won't turn anymore.

"That's it?" To me, it seems like it should have been a more complicated process.

"Water's off. What size wrench do you have?" He gestures to where I'm still gripping the cold metal in my hand.

"I dunno. It fit earlier, though."

His face pales. "Earlier?"

"It was leaking a little earlier. The video I watched to fix it said the bolt might have just been loose, so I tried tightening it, and the leak stopped for a while."

"Jesus." He scrubs his hands over his face and sighs. "Let's go check it out. I'm assuming you want to watch this, too?"

"Yup." I put on my most winning smile, which usually gets me what I want, but he just frowns and moves past me, taking the stairs slowly. His earlier stiffness was getting more severe.

"Are you sure you're okay? If you slipped on the ice, you might feel okay now, but I can tell you all the terrible things that might have happened. Trust me, slips and falls are one of the most common lawsuits we see in the winter, so I've seen file upon file of medical records."

"I'm fine. I just need to keep moving."

Men.

I don't know what gives it away, maybe there's a hint of pain in his voice, but he's hurting more than he's telling me. I know it. He attempts to move more carefully when we climb the second set of stairs, but he doesn't fool me now that I've caught on to it.

Relief fills me when we reach the bedroom and the pipe is no longer spurting water. Thank god Caleb got here quickly because the towels were already losing the battle with the flood.

"Goddammit," he grumbles, staring at the mess. "This is exactly what I don't need."

Deciding it was best to give him a minute, I go to the other bathrooms and regather all the towels, bringing them in for a second round of cleanup.

When I come back, he's on his hands and knees near the sink. I make some noise so I don't scare him; the last thing I want is for him to clunk his head, too.

"I brought these." I lift the towel pile and then lay them over the wet spots on the floor again.

"There's a wet vac downstairs," he says.

"Well, towels are easier to carry up and down the stairs. Plus, the dryer makes it nice and toasty, especially in this cold weather." I go about my business with no further comments from him.

He sighs, and I kneel next to him, peering at the mystery of the leaky pipe. "Figure out what's wrong yet?" I ask in a neutral tone. The last thing I want to do is piss him off and start an argument.

"I think it's the ring seal. I never replaced those. They get brittle in the cold and crack easily." He sits back on his heels and tries hard to hide a wince. "When you tightened it earlier, it crushed it more. That's why it got worse."

"Oh." Guilt swamps me, and I wait for him to say something mean.

"I don't have the part on hand, but at least it's an easy fix. The hardware store will have one that I can go pick up today." He falls silent while he studies the wooden floor. "I'm more worried about how much water soaked through."

I grimace. "It was dripping from the ceiling downstairs earlier. That's why I noticed it to begin with."

"Goddammit," he grumbles, his words tinged with exhaustion. I wonder just how many problems he's had this winter. Nore made it sound like it's been rough.

"What would you have to do if it was serious?" I almost don't want to hear the answer.

"Tear up the floor and maybe part of the ceiling. Drywall. Either way, I'm gonna have to figure out some way to add insulation so this doesn't happen again."

I hate to see him look so resigned.

"And if it wasn't serious?"

He smiles without humor. "Then I'd be very, very lucky for once." He stands up and offers me a hand. I almost don't take it, but I think he'd get offended if I refused. "I assume you're going to want to come to the hardware store with me?"

I study him for a moment, not sure what to make of his congenial mood.

"If you don't mind."

"You'll have to change. Otherwise, you'll freeze outside. I'll go get the truck warmed up. Meet you in ten minutes?"

"Sounds like a plan."

I'VE SEEN MORE of Caleb this last week than I did in the first two. It's like, after the pipe incident, some sort of barrier broke between us. If I didn't stop to think about it too much, it felt as if we were back to where we started in the spring. Before everything went to hell.

We replaced the pipe part together, and the next morning, I found him on my doorstep, knocking and waiting for me to answer. He asked if he could come in to make sure the pipe held up. We were polite for the fifteen minutes he lingered in the front entryway before leaving. He turned up again this morning like a miraculous delivery angel, carrying a steaming hot thermos of black coffee.

Whenever I watch him, I notice that he still holds himself with an unnatural stiffness. I haven't wanted to bring it up again, afraid to break the tentative truce we had formed. Plus, I could be imagining things. Maybe I'm just searching for anything wrong with him so I can keep my tumultuous emotions in balance.

I worry about him far more than I should. When I'm upstairs in the lighthouse, I try to glimpse his cabin, hoping to see him moving around or catch him sneaking into the guest house to clean. He's not expecting me to watch him, so he won't try to hide anything.

Knowing he's hurting, I take care of more of my messes than usual and start leaving notes, letting him know I can do my laundry. Despite the extra daily chores, I can feel the cabin fever kicking in again. I've been here for three weeks now and have yet to leave the property other than to go to the hardware store with Caleb.

Maybe that's why I tried cooking this casserole. I thought it'd be a good idea to share it with him and a good way to say thank you for all of his help. And the unexpected civility.

I don't know if the recipe will turn out, but he brought all the ingredients I needed. The original recipe is written to serve a family of six, but I don't scale it down. Leftovers are good, but I don't want that much, so sharing it with Caleb is the most simple, logical solution.

When it's ready, I bundle up in my winter gear and pick my way along the path to Caleb's cabin. I knock on the door and wait, thankful for the hot dish to help keep my fingers warm, even through my thick gloves.

I hear talking inside, and worry flashes through me that I've disrupted a guest. No one's been coming or going, so maybe it's just a phone call.

Caleb opens the door, eyebrow raised in question.

"I brought dinner. If you're hungry." He stares, and I ramble on. "To say thank you for showing me how to do everything and taking me along to get the parts." *And for actually being nice to me.* I don't say the last part since it makes me feel small and pathetic. I should be used to men being disappointed in me since that seems like all I ever get from my dad.

"I could eat." He lingers in the doorway, looking only mildly like he bit into a lemon. "Would you like to stay?"

"I—" I hesitate, waiting to see if he'll take back the invitation or let it stand. "Sure."

"You're not allergic to cats, are you?"

"Ah, no." I wrinkle my nose in confusion. "Why?"

He glances down, and I see the biggest, fluffiest cat I've ever seen being held back by Caleb's foot. He's peering outside with a yearning expression that makes me think that, at some point, he must have lived outside and liked it.

"Oh. Hi there." I don't know how I didn't notice the giant feline immediately because he's adorable.

"Monica, meet Sherman. Sherman, meet Monica. Be nice."

I don't know if the reminder is for the cat or me or more directed at himself. Caleb steps back, pushing the cat with him, and I step inside his cabin.

7

CALEB

Monica Price is in my cabin, and she's making cooing sounds at Sherman.

I wasn't sure what to expect when I opened my door to find her on my front porch, but it wasn't her throwing herself on the floor to befriend my antisocial cat. To be fair, he also looks skeptical about her advances. He tends to be suspicious of overenthusiastic attention, and she's giving him an abundance of it.

"You are so handsome. I bet you just love this weather." She makes a kissing sound and wiggles her fingers toward him in an effort to entice him to come closer.

"He likes it for a minute, but then he remembers his feet get cold and wants me to shut the door right away."

Her beaming smile causes a stutter in my heart. "Isn't that the way it is with all cats?"

I make a noncommittal sound and take the warm casserole dish she thrust into my hands to the kitchen, setting it on top of the stove and digging out the least ugly plates from my mismatched collection.

She surprised me in a good way this week. She insisted on helping and trying to take care of things herself, and I thought she was joking at first. When I call her princess, it's not just because she looks like one. Most of the time, she acts like one too.

But she wasn't afraid to get dirty, and she washed all the towels without complaint. Twice.

Now she's bringing me dinner to say thank you for including her and showing her basic kindness. It makes me feel like chewed gum stuck to the bottom of someone's shoe for the way I've been treating her. My therapist, not so subtly, pointed out that it might be because of the way she invades all my thoughts and makes me feel things.

I do my best to avoid that.

Maybe he's right. Maybe there's more to her than I'm allowing myself to see.

It felt right to show her how to fix the pipes. I can't deny that I've been craving her presence, and now that I've let myself bask in it, all I can think about is getting more.

It's how I felt when we first met.

Could I have misunderstood the conversation I overheard at the hospital? Listening to her on the phone with her father erased all my delusions that she's anything other than a stuck-up, spoiled brat.

But she isn't acting like that now, and hasn't acted like that since she's been here. Plus, she said she's avoiding her dad. Whatever is going on, it's clear I don't have the complete story.

Maybe I can put aside my prejudices for the night and try to get to know the real her a little more.

When I go back to the living area, she's coaxed Sherman into her lap, which he never lets me do. Once in a while, he'll humor me by sitting next to me. Matt's the only other person he'll let hold him for an extended period.

I scowl at my fickle cat. "My table is in the kitchen if you want to eat in there?"

"Works for me." She smiles and dislodges Sherman from his new throne. He glares at me as if I'm responsible for his diminished comfort. "I probably should have asked if you had any allergies or hated anchovies or something."

If I hadn't been getting all her groceries for her, I would've blanched in fear. But I know there aren't any anchovies anywhere on the property. "I'll eat pretty much anything. Especially if I don't have to make it."

Her demeanor softens, and I realize with a jolt that she was waiting for me to say something asinine. Guilt and shame swirl in my belly, and I can already hear my therapist saying, "I told you so," when I tell him about this.

She follows me into the kitchen and smiles when she sees that I've set my little table. I don't have anything fancy, but it's all clean, efficient, and serviceable.

I bite back a comment about it not being what she's used to because she doesn't seem to care. She settles herself in the seat nearest to the wall, and I motion toward her plate. "Big slice?"

"Yes, thank you." She hands me her plate and surveys my kitchen. Just having her here is a ray of sunshine on an otherwise dull day, as cliché as that sounds. She looks happy, and I can't remember the last time I was. I wish I could be so cheerful about something as simple as someone dishing up dinner for me.

Turning my back to her and moving to the stove, I use a spatula to pull out a sizable chunk of whatever casserole she's put together. There's cheese, tomato sauce, and pasta, so it has to be good. The little kid in me notices the tiny, sliced-up vegetables hidden in the mixture.

I pass her plate back to her and grab mine, repeating the process. “Water alright?” I set my plate down and wait.

“Of course.” She smiles and unfolds the napkin I set out, settling it in her lap with precise movements.

Feeling out of place in my own home is unsettling. She’s so delicate and refined compared to my rugged and well-used decor. It’s an uncomfortable reminder of our different backgrounds. Even if she has been eager to learn how to do some home repairs, she’s still the daughter of a politician and a doctor and used to nice things.

Words escape me when I sit back down, but she starts eating, so I follow her lead. A majority of the meal passes in silence, but it’s not awkward. We both eat hungrily, her making some cooing sounds at Sherman when he wanders in and plops himself in the middle of the rug.

After we’re finished, she helps me clean up without being asked and even starts washing the dishes while I cover the casserole. I think she’ll want to take the leftovers home with her, but when I try to give the dish back, she makes a scoffing sound. “Please. It’s for you. Besides, casseroles always taste better the second day.”

Not wanting to argue with her for once, I nod in thanks and clear out a space in the fridge. She doesn’t linger after we’re done, already slipping into her coat and shoes. I’m half tempted to offer to walk her back to the house, but that would make this feel like more than it was. I content myself with watching from my window until I see the lights turn on.

The next day, I stare at the intimidating amount of casserole left and, on a whim, send her a message asking if she'd like to come over for dinner again. I enjoyed her company last night. There wasn't any pressure to make small talk or for it to be anything but sharing food.

Yes! I'm so bored. Been working all day and now my back feels like it's stuck in one position.

I wince, intimately acquainted with the hardships of back pain. It also reminds me I haven't done my PT exercises today. I have an appointment coming up next week, and they can always tell when I've been slacking.

What time should I come over?

If I delay her a few minutes, I can get the stretches done, which should help stave off the stiffness that sets in at the end of the day.

Twenty minutes?

I pop the casserole in the oven to warm up and run through the stretching routine. Except now I'm rushing it and pushing too hard. Halfway through the first set of exercises, I feel a pop, and then the slow, spreading pain that lets me know I've done something wrong.

Fuck. This is not what I need right now.

I stop stretching and immediately get an ice pack to keep the swelling under control. I have a prescription for a painkiller, but I try to only use it as a last resort. I've heard too many horror stories of people using them and then not being able to stop.

A knock disrupts my groaning, and I hobble toward the front door, Sherman already waiting for it to open.

"Caleb, hi. What happened?" Monica's usually beautiful and sunny expression morphs into a frown when she sees me holding the ice pack.

"Something popped. Not a big deal." I step aside to let her in, but instead of making herself comfortable, she circles around behind me, moves the ice pack aside, and lifts my shirt up.

"Hey!"

"I knew you got hurt." She comes back around, and I straighten out my clothes. "Do you need me to run into the clinic with you? That bruising looks terrible."

Thank god she didn't notice the scars. They lace across the opposite side of my back from the bruising. Thankfully, I didn't land on my bad side when I slipped on the ice the other day.

"It's nothing, already getting better. The more colorful it gets, the more it's healing." She looks dubious, and I keep talking to distract her. "Food's in the oven. I might need some help to lift it out." I'm going to be lucky if I can get my pants off without killing myself tonight.

"Of course. Hi, Sherman." She bends down when he lets out a plaintive howl. "I'm sorry I was ignoring you."

She scoops him up and carries him into the kitchen with her.

The whole thing feels very domestic. Monica makes herself at home in the kitchen, settling Sherman on the chair and pulling out dishes and utensils for dinner.

I shouldn't help with anything until the ice starts working, so I sit in the chair across from Sherman and quietly watch her, listening to her inane chatter with my cat, who is also watching her every move.

He's not used to having people over, and he's not typically fond of strangers. It took Matt the better part of a month to win him over. Before I realize it, food appears in front of me, and Monica takes the empty chair between Sherman and me.

Dinner passes too quickly, and after she leaves, the house feels empty and dark.

I call the emergency number for my doctor and make an appointment for two days from now. Looks like I might have to dip into the painkillers after all.

"TAKE IT EASIER." Doctor Black glares at me. He's taller than me and bulkier, but he's the gentlest person I've ever met, so his stern warning doesn't have the effect that he's hoping for.

"I know, but I had things to do."

He cuts me off. "And I heard you've been selectively doing your PT exercises."

"To be fair, they are the reason I'm here." I raise an eyebrow in challenge.

"You're here because you haven't been doing them every day, and you were rushing. You've got to keep your head in the game with this, Caleb. If something happens, you could lose even more feeling. And because of where the scar tissue is solidifying, you're looking at limited mobility, if not complete loss of feeling."

I know my diagnosis and hate it. One stupid accident in a training exercise and a photo op sidelined me when two tours overseas didn't. "I know, Doc. I'll do better."

"Do better." He checks some notes on his computer. "It looks like you've been keeping up with your therapy sessions, at least. Are they going well?"

At first, I resisted the idea of seeing a therapist, not believing I needed one, but I've come to enjoy the appointments. If only because they got me away from home. "I think so. He's been helping me address some of my reactive behaviors that get me in the most trouble."

Doctor Black nods in agreement. "And have you given any more thought to coming to one of our support group meetings? I know Green Bay is a bit of a hike, but there's a group that meets in Sturgeon Bay every week."

Group therapy sessions are not something I am interested in at all. In the grand scheme of things, I've been very lucky. Compared to other veterans, I had two easier tours. Nothing big happened.

"I'm gonna pass on that."

"At least think about it. I know it'd be good for you."

I nod, taking the orders that the doc printed out and standing carefully. He did some laser therapy and got me in to see the chiropractor to help ease the misalignment. It was a lucky chance that kept it from being anything worse.

On my way out to the parking lot of the veteran's hospital, I pass room after room of patients. I don't know how the doctors and nurses do it. Every day, they work as hard as they can, but they can't keep up with the demand.

My mood plummets on the drive home, and even though Sherman is there waiting for me, I don't really want to go back to my cabin and be alone. I park the truck in front of the guest house, approaching the door and knocking with no small amount of hesitation. It's midday, and I know Monica mentioned that she could start working remotely now.

I don't hear her approaching, so when she opens the door, I startle, straightening with a quick jerk that sends spasms of pain across my back.

"Caleb. You alright?"

It still amazes me she's concerned about my well-being despite the way our relationship deteriorated. "Bad doctor's appointment. Mind if I come in?"

"Of course." She steps aside, and I step close to her, pausing for a moment as all sorts of thoughts bombard my head. Good god, she smells fantastic, and she looks warm and cozy in a chunky, oversized sweater and leggings. She's piled her hair on top of her head and has a pair of readers perched on top of the bun-like knot.

Shut it down, Caleb. It's not like you can do anything about it right now, anyway.

"You went to the doctor? What did they say?" She doesn't seem to notice my wayward thoughts.

"Just aggravated an old injury I thought was on the mend."

"That can be frustrating." She lingers by the reception desk, not sure what to do with me.

"Would you mind if I just hung out for a little while? My therapist says I shouldn't isolate myself when I'm feeling like this."

Shock colors her cheeks. "You're seeing a therapist? When did that happen?"

I lower my gaze, studying the grain of the hardwood floor. "Just after Halloween."

She lets out a little "Oh," and I look up, noticing how wide her eyes are and the way her mouth gapes open in surprise. Her reaction isn't judgmental like I'm always afraid it will be, and there's a distinct undercurrent of pride in her expression. "You want to come sit in the living area?"

"I'm not interrupting your work, am I?"

"No, it seems I'm more productive away from the office. I've gotten almost all my work done for this week, so I'm trying to pace myself since Naia's still not letting me do more."

"Alright." We sit on the two overstuffed couches, and I look around, noting how neat she is. I don't know if she's this way at home, too, but it seems like a character trait we both share. What does surprise me is the chess set sitting on the table, the pieces arranged in mid game. "You play?" I ask, studying the layout.

"My grandma taught me. My brother and I loved it after she explained that it was just like war." She smiles fondly at the memory. "We were always trying to beat each other."

"Mind if I play the blacks?"

She looks at the board, noting that black is already at a disadvantage with fewer pieces and the remaining ones in defensive positions. "If you want. Otherwise, we can start a new game."

"No, this is fine." The challenge of evening things out will give me something to think about. By the time we finish the first match and then another, I'm feeling more in control of my mood. No longer having an excuse to stay, I head out, driving my truck back over to the cabin and wishing for a message inviting me back for dinner.

8

MONICA

Caleb is still being nice. It makes me wonder if the therapy he's mentioned is helping that much. It also makes me wonder what he went through that made him treat people the way he does. Or if not all people, at least me since he seems to get along fine with everyone else.

Matt mentioned Caleb was in the military, although Caleb himself hasn't talked about that at all, and I don't feel comfortable bringing it up.

We've developed a routine. He still makes himself scarce during the day, doing things around the property and hanging out at his cabin while I'm also busy. We meet up after we finish for the day. Most evenings, I go over to his house to cuddle with Sherman, or he comes to the guest house, plays a few games of chess, and has dinner. In a bid to combat my cabin fever, I've been trying more and more ambitious recipes. Caleb hasn't complained yet, so either I'm a much better cook than I believed or he's got an iron stomach.

It's also shown me how much I enjoy taking care of

myself. Since I've been here, I've tried much harder to delegate specific, healthy work times and dive into activities that interest me, like cooking. When I go back to my real life, I'll have to keep this up.

Although, when I go back, I also won't have anyone to share my meals with.

Part of me is eager to get back to work. I love the hustle and bustle of the office and having a solid daily routine. But another part hates how much I've let my career consume my life. Something is going to have to change, or I'm afraid I'll turn into another version of my father.

The slower pace of life here isn't something I thought I'd enjoy. It's reminding me that I need to find a balance. Maybe that's what's been lacking in my life.

It was less obvious before last spring. Alana was there with me. She took care of me and made sure I got out, had fun, and blew off some steam. Without her, I went from work to home and back again without a variation in that routine.

In some ways, Caleb has been filling her role in my life, odd as that may sound. Except I never slept with Alana or got into the horrendous fights that I did with Caleb.

With a sigh, I set aside the contract I'm working on and stand, stretching my back and deciding I needed to move a little. Time for my excursion to the lighthouse and its daily stair-climbing challenge.

It's warmer out today, so I don't bundle up in as many layers as I usually do. Instead, I throw on my lighter jacket and walking shoes. When I reach the lighthouse, I see the visitor area lights are already on and rush in, worried that I forgot to turn them off the last time I was here.

I burst in and nearly scare Caleb off a ladder where he's

fiddling with something on the ceiling. I don't know if he's painting or spackling or doing some other handy thing, but the ladder teeters, and I rush forward, slamming down the side that's lifting off the ground so it's stable.

"Jesus, you're going to kill me," he half shouts, and for a second, I think we're returning to pre-Halloween, asshole Caleb. But he shakes his head, and I watch him take deep breaths, clenching and unclenching his hands.

"You okay?" I let go of the ladder slowly so I can make sure it doesn't fall on top of both of us.

"Yeah, just gave me a start." And then he smiles.

It's the first time I've seen him smile since we met, and it makes him look five years younger. His normally stiff expression softens with laugh lines and a dimple. My fingers press into my chest, where my heart is beating harder than it should be.

"Adrenaline sure gives you a rush." He chuckles, and I stare while he climbs down the ladder and places both feet firmly on the ground. He dusts his hands off against his pants and makes white smears across the denim.

I blurt out the first question that comes to mind, needing to get my thoughts off how handsome he looks. "What were you doing up there, anyway?"

"Touching up a few spots. It's warm enough with the heater running that I wanted to take care of it before the cracks get worse. I'll paint it tomorrow or the next day." He must see the question on my face because he sighs, and his lips quirk again. "Yes, you can help."

I let out a squeal and clap my hands.

"You are the strangest person I've ever met." He shakes his head and folds the ladder, moving it into a storage room that's half hidden behind a display case.

"I'm so bored. Everything seems new and exciting after you've been staring at contracts all day."

"I can only imagine." He comes back out, coat already on. "I'll head out and leave you to it, then."

A sudden idea strikes me. "You said it's nicer out today. Do you have anything else to do outside? I'm getting a little sick of climbing stairs for exercise." He studies me for a moment, eyes dropping to my mesh sneakers and then back up to my jacket. "I'll change. I swear it won't take long."

His eyebrow raises in question. "You don't even know what I have planned yet."

"It doesn't matter. If it gets me out of the house, I'm all in."

He laughs, and I get so caught in the sound—deep and rich and so unlike what I expect from him—that I freeze. "Alright. Go get changed while I finish putting this stuff away."

I bolt out of the door because suddenly he's the guy I caught feelings for last spring. The one who could get me so outside of my head that I forgot about all the expectations constantly placed on me and was very much able to enjoy our time together.

I don't know what to do about that. Protective instincts rear up, wanting to shield my heart from all the confusion and hurt I battled before. Hope and want push back, yearning for a connection with someone.

I DAWDLE in the house and attempt to rein in my wayward emotions. The only thing that gets me back outside is the realization that Caleb might take off without me. To do what, I'm still not sure, but I know I don't want to miss it.

Sure enough, he's waiting on the deck, watching the distant waves on the lake. The sun is out today, so it's not as steel gray as it is when it's overcast, but it still looks vast and powerful. "I bet you never get sick of this view," I murmur, not wanting to disrupt the peaceful silence.

"No, I don't. But the woods are just as beautiful. In the spring and fall, there's so much color and life."

I step up next to him and gaze out at the lake. Even though I grew up in Green Bay, the wide open expanse of water still makes me nervous. Our family isn't big into boating, so I haven't ventured further than the marina.

"So. What are we doing?"

He grins with a mischievous glint in his eye. That's what makes me think he's laying down a challenge. "Well, as you've seen, I have a fireplace, and I need wood."

I can't help the snort that escapes. One thing is for sure: Caleb doesn't need any help in the wood department.

Shut those thoughts down, Price.

"We've got to haul in a tree that came down this fall. Then you can help me get it ready to chop." He pulls something out of his coat pocket and hands it to me. "These should fit you."

It's a pair of leather gloves that still look brand new. I'm glad I thought to put on a thin pair of gloves because they add an extra layer of insulation inside the cold, stiff leather as I slip them on. "Should work."

"Great. Ever been on a four-wheeler before?" He steps to the side, and I see a huge ATV parked on the drive, a small trailer hitched up behind it, presumably to haul the wood from wherever it is to Caleb's cabin.

"Nope."

"Well, the day will be full of unknown adventures."

I follow him toward the machine, and he climbs on first, scooting forward so I can sit behind him. Twisting my arms around his chest shouldn't feel as intimate as it is, with the dual layers of our coats and winter clothes between us. But I can feel the heat radiating from his body, and the clean, crisp air mixes with the musky scent that seems to naturally belong to Caleb.

Combined with the vibration of the motor, I'm feeling some kind of way before we even reach the tree line.

Thankfully, Caleb doesn't seem to catch on.

"How much of this is your land?" I holler over the sound of the engine and wind. It seems like we've been driving for a long time.

"We're on my neighbor's property right now. I've got just over four acres."

It's another five minutes of bumping down the snow-covered path before I see the large outline of a tree in the snow. I know he's been out this way before because tire marks carve through the snow, but I'm not expecting the tree to already be sectioned off into smaller chunks. A secret part of me was looking forward to watching him swing an axe.

"I might need your help with a few of the larger chunks. My doctor said I need to take it a little easier."

He still hasn't talked about what happened, just the same line about an old injury. My mouth opens, the urge to ask him about it strong, but I push it back down.

"I can do that." I do CrossFit occasionally. Maybe it'll be just like the tire flips. At least, that's what I tell myself.

We don't start with the biggest piece, but I'm already

struggling. There are at least half a dozen chunks, plus all the other smaller branches to load up. My only comfort is that Caleb looks like he's not doing so well, either.

"Why don't we cut these down smaller so we don't kill ourselves?" I ask. There's a chainsaw in the trailer bed, so we might as well use it.

"Yeah. I think I'm going to have to."

Yay! Chainsaw time.

"Before you ask, no, you can't use it. It's almost half as big as you, and it can give a nasty kick if you hit a knot in the wood."

"That's fine because I wasn't going to ask. I defended an injury lawsuit a few years ago, so I know all the statistics." That case left some gruesome pictures burned into my brain.

He nods, and I watch him prepare the chainsaw and start it up. It looks way too easy when he saws through the first chunk. When he moves on to the second, I try to see if I can move the first one by myself.

No dice. The thing doesn't even budge. I guess this means I need to add some strength training into my routine because I am not at all as strong as I thought. Maybe Andrea will have some tips.

Caleb cuts through another chunk and then several more until he gets all the larger pieces cut in half. When he shuts the chainsaw off and puts it away, I ask, "Why don't you ask the guys to come help with this? Bret would love it. It's like outdoor weightlifting."

Caleb's shaking his head before I finish speaking. "I don't want to bother them with something as simple as this. Plus, they're all busy with businesses to run and significant others to pay attention to."

"And you don't?" It bothers me that he doesn't see himself as worthy of their help or even as their equal. He owns his own business, too, even if it's in its first year. The only difference is the significant other part. Unless he has a hidden lady friend stashed somewhere.

"I certainly do not have a girlfriend if that's what you're hinting at." He motions toward the nearest chunk of wood, and I bend down to help lift it. "Make sure you lift with your legs." His voice is clipped, and I obey instinctively.

I guess the subject is closed. Not that I've ever paid attention to that particular social cue. "You could have a boys' night. You know, do manly things, drink beers, whatever it is you four do when you're together."

We lift the wood over the side and set it in the trailer so we don't damage the bottom. Caleb works to maneuver it so we can fit the rest of the pieces in.

"Would this be like one of your girls' nights? I've heard about the amount of wine involved. I was at Steve's the last time he got a call to come pick Andrea up."

I shrug, unashamed of my friends. "They're fun. Plus, the girls have all been so kind and accepting." My words trail off, and I get stuck in memories of a time when it was just me and Alana.

"Why do I sense some kind of but there?" We work together to get two more pieces in the trailer before I answer, and I realize Caleb is much more patient than I've given him credit for. Not once does he push for a response. He just waits, giving me space to think.

"I wasn't in a great place after everything that happened last spring. Alana and I were best friends for years, more like sisters in some ways. When everything came to light and she got arrested, it left a huge void. One that I'm still not sure how to fill."

Caleb watches me, hands on his hips. "She was an assistant DA, right?"

I nod. "I feel so ashamed that I didn't figure out what she was doing. That she almost got Andrea and Nore hurt haunts my dreams. I wound up cutting myself off from everyone." I bend down to pick up a few of the larger branches and walk back to the trailer. Caleb stays where I left him, looking down at the ground. "Sarah was one of the first to barge in and drag me out of my shell. Nore and Andrea weren't very far behind her."

More wood piles up in the trailer, and we're down to just sticks and a few smaller twigs.

"I did that too after I got discharged. Matt and Steve would go months without hearing from me."

"Huh. Another thing we have in common. Who'd have thought?" I smile and start picking up the rest of the branches so we can get back to the cabin and finish unloading.

"Lord help us," Caleb mutters under his breath but doesn't say anything else.

I spend the rest of our time in the woods trying to figure out if he's mad about that or some other, more nuanced emotion.

THE NEXT MORNING, I run into Caleb again, only this time he's heading for the guest house instead of somewhere else on the property.

"Hey. I was thinking about what you said last night." He

looks almost sheepish, like he's done something wrong. "We should have everyone out for a get-together, maybe at the end of the week?"

"Really?" The idea sounds great to me, but I'm beginning to get to know Caleb, and being around that many people at once is not his idea of fun. He's taken me to the hardware store twice now, and he always gets antsy when there's a crowd of people.

"I think it'd be good practice for larger groups." He motions toward the guest house. "You know, weddings and things like that. If we give Andrea enough notice, maybe she'll bring some food, too."

"Ah." I lightly slug him in the arm. "I see your real motives now. You're sick of my attempts at cooking."

He laughs again, and my heart does a little flip. "I need to reach out more. It's the guys who call me, not the other way around."

This, more than anything else, makes me think he's taking his therapy seriously. He's acting so differently than he has for the last year. He's listening and thinking and trying to step out of his comfort zone more often.

"Then let's do it. Do you want to call everyone, or should I?"

9

CALEB

We have the party at the guest house since it's bigger, and that's where any future events will be. Monica asked if I could come help move her file boxes into the office so we could use the chairs in the living room.

I was also hoping we could do a little cleaning, too, since, truth be told, she hasn't let me do my usual routine; I'm itching, thinking about all the places that might have gotten missed. Even though it's just our friends coming over, I want it to look nice.

Like it would if they were paying guests.

Word of mouth is everything, and even though I know my friends would talk me up no matter what, I want them to have the experience to back it up.

I open the door without knocking and surprise her with a handful of files in her arms. She jumps, the files fall, and papers fly all over the front hallway. "Shit." Without hesitating, she crouches and starts gathering them up, giving me an unintended view down the front of her loose shirt.

Lately, I've been having a harder time ignoring the feelings that drew me to her when we first met. She is a gorgeous woman who any man would want, but she also has high standards. I felt privileged that things wound up where they did in the hotel room last spring.

And now, after getting to know her more, I'm having a hard time reconciling the way I let things fall apart so quickly with the more complete picture of who she is. My therapist told me I should talk to her about it, clear the air, and maybe start over. Maybe we could even try out this whole, healthy adult relationship thing.

"Sorry, that was my fault." I crouch down and gather the papers nearest me. We meet in the middle of the hallway, and I hand her the stack I shuffled together. "Need help putting them back in order?"

She smiles, but it's wobbly. "A job for another day. Thanks for helping me move this stuff. And volunteering to help clean. I don't know why I told Andrea I'd make appetizers." Her eyes aren't as bright as they normally are.

With a start, I realize she's nervous. I assumed things like this would be what she's used to. Parties. Hosting friends. "Everything you've made for dinner has been great, and you know I'd tell you if it wasn't."

She snorts, her nose wrinkling. "I'm sure you would."

We stand there, lost in the moment. She's smiling at me, and I'm unsure what to do next but don't want to ignore our growing connection. "Can I ask you a question?"

She nods, wariness clouding her eyes.

"Why didn't you stay with your grandma? Why come here?" They're questions that have been bothering me for a while. I know her grandmother lives out in the country in a fancy cabin.

"I don't really know." She looks down, and I watch her fingers twist together, a nervous habit I've never noticed before. "It's just... when the girls said I could get a break from my dad if I came here, I latched onto it. He's been so overbearing, and if I was at Grandma's, he'd have free rein to come and go as he pleased, inundating me with his demands of my life."

There's more to it than that, but I'll take this answer for now, knowing exactly what her dad can be like. "Can I ask you another question?" This one is far more dangerous.

She nods.

"If we could start over, pretend we just met here and now, do you think you'd give me another chance?"

Her head shoots up, eyes wide and jaw dropped, but no words come out. A light flush creeps across her cheeks, and she brings her hand up to her mouth, so I don't know if she's smiling or frowning.

"You don't have to answer that if you don't want to," I rush to say.

She straightens and looks me in the eye. "If you'd just met me now, what would you have done?"

I answer without missing a beat. "Tried to hit on you."

She snorts, and some of the stiffness leaves her shoulders. "Yeah, I'd give you another chance." Her smile is soft and tentative, like the first time a flower's petals open in the spring.

I relax and feel my lips quirk in response. "I'm sorry I acted like such an ass." She looks like she wants to interrupt me, probably to probe for a deeper explanation, but I can't give her that yet because I don't even know what I'd been thinking. "Let's get ready for this party."

She gives me a funny look but doesn't stop me from going into the living room and moving her files to the office.

"YOU TWO MAKE FRIENDS AGAIN?" Steve asks. We're parked in opposite corners of one of the big couches, Matt is sprawled in the armchair next to us, and Bret is lying across the length of the other couch.

"In a way." I don't even have to ask who he's talking about. I'm doing a terrible job of keeping my attention off of her. The ladies have gathered around the kitchen island, but they left the door open so we can still see them.

"You're not hooking up with her, are you?" Matt sits up, looking more concerned than I believed he could be. "She's been struggling, and the last thing she needs is more heartbreak."

"You sound like your fiancé," I fire back with more vehemence than I intended. "Sorry. That was harsh." The doc keeps saying if I recognize when I've reacted defensively and acknowledge that, it's a sign I'm using my skills.

And I definitely know I said something wrong. Steve's giving me a sour look, and even Bret's raised an eyebrow in question. Matt, to his credit, doesn't react with more than a nod. Sadly, they've gotten used to my angry outbursts these last few years.

"You look like you're doing better since Monica came here," Bret mentions, lounging on the sofa.

Steve and Matt both look at him like he's crazy but turn back to study me.

"You do look more relaxed," Matt says.

"Yeah, you're not scowling all the time, and you're actually talking in full sentences," Steve chimes in.

"I've been going to therapy," I mumble, not sure if I'm ready to admit it to my friends or not, but knowing it has to come out sometime.

Matt and Steve have known me longer than Bret, but he's the one who speaks up first. "That's good, man. Sarah's been going too, and she says it's really helping."

"Nore and I still go every month," Matt adds.

It's reassuring to know that none of them is passing judgment. It's a fear I've always had that people would assume something is wrong or broken or that I'm weak and not able to do things on my own.

Before we can get any deeper into the discussion, the ladies come streaming in. Each one partners up with their significant other, leaving Monica with the open space between Andrea and me. She sits down, but I notice she's careful to maintain some space between us. Compared to the other women, she's not as relaxed either. She's talked about how hard it is for her to make friends, and I wonder if she still feels out of place or if she's just still nervous about hosting everyone.

After hearing Monica talk more about Alana and learning more about her relationship with her dad, I can see how this situation could push a few of her triggers. It also helped me understand the ladies' dynamic better. What I saw as haughtiness before was just Monica trying to find her footing. Despite her job and the outgoing public persona she projects, she's much more introverted than people realize.

I lean over so the others won't hear. "Are you doing okay?"

She startles but nods, a half-smile pulling up the corner of her lips. "Yeah, sorry. It's just weird being one of the few single ones in a friend group of couples."

"I know what you mean." The mix of loneliness and jealousy lives alongside my happiness for my friends.

"What are you two whispering about over there?" Nore says just loud enough to get everyone's attention. Six sets of eyes focus on us, and I notice Monica's deep blush.

"How weird you all are." I smile to soften what could have been a sharp rebuke. "We feel like a pair of cool single people at an old married couple's party."

Andrea snorts. "Don't worry, we're not getting married anytime soon. But luckily, this one knows I'm possessive enough to never let him get too far away."

"That's very true." Steve tips his beer toward her and keeps a straight face. "She can be terrifying." He jumps and glares at Andrea, who must have just goosed him.

Laughter fills the room, and we talk long into the night. By the time everyone leaves, I feel more settled than I have in a long time. This was a good idea, not only for me but also for Monica. She looks happier, more animated. I know she's getting stir-crazy being out here all the time, and I wonder how long she'll want to stay.

The thought of her leaving is like a pinprick in the balloon of my good mood, and I excuse myself as soon as we finish cleaning everything up. My walk back to my house is slow, and I stop to look at the sky. The cloudless night reveals almost every star, and I gaze at them, a feeling of emptiness washing over me.

"CALEB." Monica's standing on my doorstep a few days after the party. We haven't talked more about what I asked her that afternoon, but I've been thinking about it nonstop. When I see her, all the ways I might convince her to come inside and spend time with me swamp my thoughts. I wouldn't care if we were just working quietly together in the same room.

Or if I'm really brave, maybe I could try to convince her to go on a date.

Then I see how much she's shivering.

"What happened?" I pull her inside and shut the door, maneuvering her toward the couch where Sherman's sprawled on his back. I shove him aside, and he leaps down and gives an angry flick of his tail. I put Monica in his spot and drape a blanket around her, then unceremoniously dump Sherman onto her lap so he can help warm her up.

"I think the furnace might have gone out." The words are semi-intelligible through the loud chattering of her teeth.

"When?" It can't have just happened. You don't get that cold that fast unless something is wrong with you.

"Sometime overnight. At first, I thought it was just the temps dropping. But then I woke up, and it wasn't getting any warmer, so I went to go check."

Shit. The heater in the guest house was installed the same year as the heater in the lighthouse. If I was lucky, maybe the same part would be the issue. Except it took over a week to get the damn thing in the mail and get it fixed.

"I'm going to get you something warm to drink and then go check. You'll be alright here for a little while."

Sherman's burrowing into her lap, and her fingers are stroking through his long hair. I wait for her to nod before heading to the kitchen. I haven't been this worried about someone for a long time. Probably not since I was overseas with my unit.

Not bothering to put the kettle on for hot water, I dump some in a coffee mug and stick it in the microwave, grabbing a few tea bags while it heats.

"I wasn't sure what flavor you might want, so I got a few." I hold them out to her, and she reaches for them, teeth still chattering and skin cold to the touch.

"You pick."

I take the fruit-flavored one that I bought on a whim—and hate—and dunk it in to steep.

"I'm going to run over and check it out. Are you going to be okay?"

She nods and, to my relief, is shivering less, too. "Feeling warmer already."

Faster than I thought possible, I get dressed and hurry along the path. I hit the front door at a jog and throw it open, taking the stairs to the basement at a near run.

If it's the same problem as the other heater, I'm going to have to break the news to her that she can't stay here. That makes the twisting ache in my chest sharpen. The thought of her leaving tears something inside me.

At that moment, I realized I didn't want to let her go. It's already going to be difficult seeing other people in the rooms she's used for the last month.

When I get to the front of the furnace, I go straight for the part that I think is malfunctioning and find it looking just as crispy and slightly blackened as the other one.

Fuck. I should have ordered an extra when the other broke, just in case.

Shutting the front and bringing up the manufacturer's

site on my phone, I order two of what I need, checking to see if there's a rush shipping option.

There isn't. Minimum of one week, probably two.

The walk back to my cabin is much slower. My steps are sluggish, and my boots feel heavier than normal.

"Did you get it working?" Monica calls from the couch when she hears the door open.

I come and sit on the couch, half turned so I'm facing her. "It's the same part that broke on the other furnace, and I can't get one here for a week. Then I'll need Matt's help to get it installed and working."

Her lips pull down in a frown, but to my relief, at least she's stopped shivering. "Oh."

The words catch in my throat, and I have to clear it before I say, "I can't let you stay there without a heater while the part is being shipped. I'm sorry."

She swallows and looks away, petting Sherman a few more times. I hate this. The thought of not seeing her every day is like a spike in my heart. What will I do at dinner every night or afterward? No more games of chess or quiet nights watching a movie together.

"What if I stayed here with you? It's just for a week, right?"

10

MONICA

My anxiety makes me feel like this is a make-or-break moment in our relationship. If he says no, then it closes the door on the connection that's been building between us. Right now, it's still fragile, and all the old, badly patched cracks are showing.

But if he says yes...

My heart is afraid to even contemplate it. Taking a chance on someone has always been a risk for me, let alone building something romantic.

"You wouldn't mind that?" He looks toward his bedroom, and I watch him swallow hard. "I'll sleep on the couch, and you can take the bed. Sherman might hog your space, but it's not bad otherwise."

To be fair, I hadn't even considered the sleeping situation when I suggested this. My idea was driven more by a desire to not leave than by any ulterior motives. "I don't want to kick you out of your bed. I can stay on the couch."

"You're not staying on the couch."

It's short and well-cushioned, but not huge. My sleep

hasn't been that great anyway, so I could make it work, but I don't want to. Not if he's offering to share. "Then I guess we'll be sharing."

His expression screws up tight, like he's struggling to find any other argument to avoid saying yes. "I'm not letting you pay for this week or next week if you still want to stay."

"That's fine." I set Sherman down on the ground and stand, folding the blanket and putting it back on the couch. "I'll go grab my stuff and bring it over."

He stands there, too stunned that he's going to have a temporary roommate to stop me from walking out the door. I can move my things by myself, but it's going to take a few trips. That'll give him some time to come to terms with our new situation.

"Wait. I'll help you."

Or maybe he's more accepting than I thought.

Staying with Caleb is enlightening. Not only because I see his daily habits, but also because it's told me more about what's going on with him than he ever has.

Yesterday, he disappeared for an hour. I thought he was working on the furnace at the guest house, but when I went to check on him, he wasn't there. The lighthouse was empty, too.

I finally found him walking up and down a trail in the woods, talking to someone on the phone. Not wanting to interrupt, I made sure I was out of earshot and stayed where I was until he was done with his call.

When I asked him who it was, he got cagey. Which only sparked my curiosity more. Turns out he talks to his therapist at least once a week, sometimes twice. I didn't know their interactions were so frequent, but I noticed how much more introspective he becomes after the call, like he's taking time to process whatever they spoke about.

Then, I discovered he does physical therapy exercises every morning and night. For what injury, I still don't know. That's something he's been firm on not telling me about when I press him.

He's also putting an incredible amount of work into getting his business up and ready for the next tourist season. While I'm out in the living room working through whatever files Naia and Alicia have sent me, he's in his office toiling away over a seemingly endless to-do list. This would be his first full year in business, and I know he's put a lot of pressure on himself to make it successful.

It seems we could both be serious workaholics when we have nothing better to do. When he emerges from the office late each afternoon, I see how carefully he moves, and I know whatever injury he's still dealing with gets aggravated from sitting in a cheap office chair all day.

So, I've taken it upon myself to help him by disrupting his office sessions. If that also gives me a break from my work, so be it.

"Caleb." I add an extra whine to my voice to get his attention. Since we've stopped sniping at each other, I've discovered he doesn't mind it so much. "I'm bored."

The chair in his office squeaks when he shifts, and I hear the wheels bumping across the hardwood floor as he scoots back. Soon, his body fills the door frame, one hand braced on the side with a slight lean that's completely unintentional but unbearably sexy. My heart does a little swoon, and I do my best to school my expression. "What do you want me to do about it?"

So far, we've avoided any discussion of a potential relationship, but I'm ready to push the issue. Sleeping next to him each night is messing with my head, especially since we found out how much sexual chemistry we have. Maybe spending more time with each other will help us get over our communication issues. "Can we go out to dinner tonight? I need to get out of here."

He straightens and steps away from the doorframe, folding his arms across his chest. "What if someone sees you? It might get back to your dad."

At this point, I really couldn't care. I've avoided him for the last five weeks, which feels like a once-in-a-lifetime gift from the universe. "Odds are low. It's winter, and we're probably two hours away from the city."

He snorts. "It's cute that you think you're that unrecognizable. Between being Paul Price Senior's daughter and all the media coverage from last spring, I'd say odds are better than fifty-fifty that someone will know who you are."

I know I'll have to talk to Dad some time, but he hasn't called yet, and I'd like to avoid this confrontation as long as I can. He's also not one to make casual conversation, so unless it's related to family business, he won't call just to see how I'm doing. I've talked to my brother a few times in the last couple of weeks, and he's made it sound like Dad's attention has turned to him anyway. The bill he and his fiancée are working on passed out of committee and will come to a floor vote soon.

If there was one thing Dad couldn't stay away from, it was a media spectacle. He always told us we needed to take advantage of good PR moments whenever possible. That, more than anything, described our lives growing up. Stilted, performative, and emotionless.

"I'll wear a disguise. Maybe steal one of your hats and a flannel."

He bursts into laughter, and his whole face changes. It's wondrous to behold his transformation from stoic to joy-filled. A part of me swells with pride that I can give him these moments of levity. "If you willingly wear one of my flannels, I'll take you out to dinner tonight. But I get to pick the place, and you can't complain."

"Deal." I agree without hesitation. I'm not even suspicious of the smirk on his face when he disappears back into his office. If he's trying to trick me into embarrassing myself, he hasn't seen my tricks with oversized shirts yet.

I can guarantee that I'm going to look good tonight. Flannel shirt or not.

Caleb's mouth pops open, and I force myself not to gloat. Instead, I project nonchalance and relaxation. "Ready to go?" My heeled boots make a satisfying clack on the floor as I cross to where he's standing by the door, coat half on, arm lifted to slip on the other sleeve.

"Uh. Yeah." His eyes do a quick up-and-down dip before his Adam's apple bobs, and he refocuses on my face. "You ready? I mean, obviously, you're ready." His words trail off, and I swear I see a tinge of red underneath his end-of-the-day scruffy cheeks.

With slow movements, I swing on my coat, revealing the hint of my midriff and the low V-neck created with the loosening of an extra button. His throat clears, and I smile, concealing my triumph as I turn away to pick up my purse. "Are you going to tell me where we're going?"

"You going to chicken out if I do?" That hint of challenge is back in his expression, and even though I should know better, I always take that bait.

"Nope."

He nods. "Well, options are limited this time of year. The Blue Ox and Florian are both closed for the season, so Cornerstone is one of the few places left open in Bailey's Harbor."

I don't spend a lot of time in the area, so I haven't heard of those places before. "Sounds good."

Another inarticulate sound of agreement comes from him, and I loop my arm through his. If my boob presses against his arm while waiting for him to open the door, so be it. He might not have called this a date, but that's definitely how I'm thinking about it.

There's a distinct pause, and a slight shake of his head seems to bring him to his senses. He holds the door open for me to step through. Sherman bids us farewell with a plaintive howl, flicks his tail, and slinks toward the bedroom.

Caleb rolls his eyes and mutters "spoiled brat" before shutting the door. Like a true gentleman, he helps me step up into his enormous truck and makes sure I'm buckled in before closing the door. I watch him jog around the hood and hop up into his seat. He turned the truck on before we came out, so it's toasty and warm, unlike the air, which took another nose dive today.

It's not too long before we're cruising down Highway 57, and Caleb stops in front of a big gray building. There's open parking on the street, so we're able to pull up close to the door. "Wait there. I'll come around." Caleb, who's been silent the whole ride, bolts from the car and races around the hood once again. If he was really mad at me, his cold shoulder might be more irritating. But I know he's not. He kept peeking over at me, his hands squeezed the steering wheel like he wasn't sure what to do with them.

He's just nervous and as out of his element as I am.

He opens my door, and for a second, my stomach flutters. My stomach never flutters. There's a slight tremor in my fingers as I loosen the seat belt, and Caleb holds out a hand to help me down. When my feet hit the ground, I look up and catch Caleb watching me. For once, his expression is unguarded. He looks a little stunned, like he can't believe this is happening.

To be honest, neither can I. After the way we treated each other for the last six months, I never thought we'd be going on a not-a-date date. I also never would have believed that we'd been peacefully cohabitating for almost a week. Or that he has a cat. Or that he's hiding so much of himself from his friends.

"You ready?" I ask, needing to break the silence and my sudden fascination with the way I can look him directly in the eye when I'm wearing my heels.

"Yeah." Low and sure. His eyes roam across my face, and he reluctantly steps back, letting me move out of the truck door so he can close it. Before I even hear the click of the lock, his arm bands across my lower back, a shade too tight to be just friends. My stomach does that swooping thing again, and I let myself lean against him, tucking my hand into his back pocket.

"Tell me about this place?" I ask as we approach the door.

His fingers flex against my side, and I can feel the heat

from his arm radiating across my back. "The building's been here for a while, but the ownership's changed a few times. It's been a bar for years now." He holds the door open for me, and I step inside, taking in the long bar top and mostly empty tables.

"Doesn't look like many people come by in the winter. I'm surprised they're still open."

"Lots of snowmobilers around here. And the locals come by enough, I suppose. Bar or table?"

"Bar." I snag his hand and tug him toward the center of the long, polished wood bar top. There are plenty of open seats, but I like the feeling of being right in the middle of the space. It's homey, but not overly so. Comfortable and not at all pretentious.

Before I can climb up onto the barstool, I feel a gentle tug on my coat sleeve. "I can take that for you." I let him help me slide it off, and he drapes it over the back of the empty chair behind us.

"Can I help you two?" The bartender comes over. He looks like he could be anywhere between forty and sixty, and I wonder how long he's worked here.

Caleb waits for me to say something first, but I'm still not sure what the protocols are. Are we drinking and having fun or just escaping the house for the night? "Hard cider." It seems like a safe option.

"New Glarus on tap," Caleb chimes in before settling himself on the stool and turning just enough so that we're able to look at each other. The local radio station is playing in the background, and the two guys sitting at the far end of the bar are doing more eating than talking, so it's the only background noise.

Caleb and I lapse into silence, glancing at each other

before settling our gazes on the bar, watching the bartender, and pretending that we're both not as confused about this as the other.

"What are we doing here?" I blurt after the drinks arrive and we've given the bartender our food order. The question hangs in the air for a beat while I take a hearty swig to hide my embarrassment.

Caleb sighs, setting his glass down carefully on the coaster so that it's centered. "We're having dinner."

I turn and bump my knee against his thigh. There's no give, just hard, lean muscle. "You know what I'm asking."

"Do you want this to be something more than just dinner?"

He doesn't look at me, and I want to grab the frustrating man by the collar and shake him. "Do you?"

"God help me, I think I do." He spins his glass on the coaster, and just when I'm about to open my mouth and lambaste him for sounding so bereaved, he keeps talking. "I don't really know what you see in me, but something's been pulling us together." He looks up, and the deep brown of his eyes snares me. "You feel it too, I think."

Helpless to say anything, I just nod and wait for him to keep talking.

"I'm afraid that if I give in to that, when you wise up and leave me, I'll be even more of a mess than I already am. It's taken me a long time to get this far, and the idea of screwing that up—" He stops and shakes his head, looking past me. "I don't even know how dating between us would work."

There are so many questions swirling around in my head and so much of his past that he still hasn't talked to me about, but the one thing I know is that I've felt that draw between us. More than I've felt with anyone else before. "My first thought when you told me I couldn't stay in the house wasn't about me having to pack up and find somewhere else to stay. It was that I didn't want to leave you."

Caleb's attention focuses back on me, and I pause, waiting for him to absorb what I'm saying. "I don't know how this would work either, but if there's one thing this last year has hammered home to me, it's that I need to make some changes. Seeing our friends find relationships has shown me how hollow my life has been. I used to fill up all my time with work, so it was easier to ignore how alone I felt. How unhappy I've become. You were the first person who made me want to reach out and take a risk on something new."

I want to touch him and establish that connection again, so I reach out and take his hand. He startles like he wasn't expecting it. My heart cracks at the idea that he might not think I see anything in him. "I'm scared too and can't guarantee what the future holds, but I want to try."

He squeezes my hand, and his lips quirk into something that looks like a smile but isn't quite all the way there. "You know I'm probably going to be an ass at some point. And I'm definitely going to react badly to something and piss you off."

"Yes." I nod, agreeing without pause. It pulls a bark of laughter out of him. "But I'm the same way. Too quick to judge and I shut down when I get angry."

"Alright then." He nods, and there's a lightness in his eyes I'm not used to seeing. Any further discussion gets cut off by our food and my growling stomach.

For the rest of the night, we talk about nothing and everything, only leaving when the bartender sends us pointed looks since everyone else left over an hour before.

Caleb holds out my coat for me, and I slip my arms inside, buttoning it up while he puts his on. With more confidence than I've felt before, I reach out and loop my arm through his, pulling him in close and laying my head on his shoulder as we walk out to the truck.

As soon as he puts the truck in drive, he takes my hand, resting our entwined fingers on the center console, thumb brushing against the back of my hand in slow swipes. The ride back is quiet, only the radio playing in the background. It's peaceful, and I'm looking forward to getting back to the house and seeing where things might go. I think Caleb's on the same page.

He looks more relaxed, too. Something eased in the way he carries himself, and I can only dare to hope that he's letting me in a little more now that we've talked things through.

When we get back, he takes a minute to feed Sherman, and I turn some music on low. I turn from the bookcase where I've propped my phone up to find Caleb standing in the kitchen doorway, watching me with a hungry look.

"Dance with me?" I hold out my hand, and he walks over, slow and purposeful, pulling me into him. I revel in the hard strength of his body and the way we seem to fit together even though I've kicked off my boots.

He keeps my right hand in his, looping his other arm around my back and tucking me against him so that my head rests just underneath his chin. His chest expands, and a soft exhale shifts my hair. I might be imagining things, but I think I feel his lips move against my hair, and I let myself go lax with happy contentment.

We sway side to side, not moving much, as one song blends into another. His hand against my back eases lower until it's nearly tucked into the back pocket of my jeans, cupping my butt and keeping our hips pressed close.

Everything in me is calling out to take him, kiss him, and move this show into the bedroom.

The blaring of my ringtone shatters the moment, and I jerk back, noticing that Caleb does the same, a wide, stunned look in his eyes.

"You going to answer that?" he asks when I don't move away from him.

I don't want to. I know who it is and that it can't be good if he's calling this late. Normally, I would still be awake, but he's supposed to be thinking I'm on a volunteer vacation helping underprivileged communities. "I don't want to."

His fingers squeeze once before he pulls away, making the choice for me. My steps feel leaden as I move to pick up the screen and swipe right. "Hi, Dad."

Caleb flinches and retreats another step, looking toward the bedroom door like he wants to run. I don't even hear Dad's first words because I'm watching Caleb wall himself off before my eyes.

11

CALEB

Of course.

Of course, Paul Price Senior would call now, just when everything is going right. Why is he calling this late, anyway? It's close to eleven, and any other sane person would be asleep this late on a Wednesday.

I can hear their muffled conversation through the bedroom door. I closed it, trying to block out the spectral presence of Monica's father. Everything inside of me wants to convince my heart that this night was a mistake, that she's just like her father, and that his calling her now proves how alike they are.

But my heart is steadfastly saying no. I'm misunderstanding the situation again. It whispers that I need to create some space and cool down before I lash out.

"Dad."

I flinch. Monica's voice is sharp and loud enough that I can hear it clearly through the door. I can only imagine what he said to make her so mad.

Knowing him, it could be anything.

Memories that I've long buried resurface, and I scrub my fingers through my hair, digging into the muscles at the back of my neck and dragging them back up my skull. I've never told Monica, but I know her father. Not well, more in passing than anything else, but it's still enough to know he's a terrible person.

He was part of a photo op with my unit before my first deployed tour. I was full of all the naïve expectations I thought I'd find overseas. I was a cocky shit, but I still tried to be a good person, paying attention to other people around me.

Senator Price did not. He and his posse barged into our barracks, complained about being there and how they needed to leave fast, and then barely acknowledged any of the people they were making pose for photos.

We were all surprised, since he was supposed to be such a nice guy. A family man who embodied Wisconsin's values. I'd written it off as him having a bad day. There could have been something important going on that he needed to take care of.

Two years later, one of my friends needed a letter of recommendation so she could pursue officer's school. She reached out to Price, but no matter what she did, she couldn't get a response from him or anyone in his office. Finally, after months of trying, she drove down to see him in person. Price was nowhere to be found, but his assistant had told her he would never recommend a woman to officer's school.

After that, I wanted nothing to do with him. He cropped up again from time to time, but I avoided him for another three years until I got hurt.

And now his daughter is staying with me.

Fucking hell, Corcoran; she's not her father.

But right now, it's too difficult to separate the two, and all I want to do is turn off the lights, crawl into bed, and pretend the last twenty minutes went a different way. I shuck off my clothes, pull on a pair of sweats, and turn off the lights.

I've gotten so used to having Monica in bed with me the past few days that now it feels empty without her. I wrestle my pillow into a lumpy shape and bury my face in it, thankful that Sherman followed me in here so at least I'm not completely alone.

There's no chance I'm sleeping yet. Not when I can hear Monica's voice, spiking in anger every so often, and the pacing thump of her footsteps on the floor back and forth across the living room. Sherman has no qualms about immediately falling asleep, and he settles into a tight ball right behind my knees.

It could be twenty minutes later or two hours when the talking stops. My heartbeat picks up in anticipation of what she'll do.

The bedroom door opens quietly, and a sliver of light flashes against the wall before she slips inside and shuts it again. With disquieting familiarity, she navigates through the dark and into the bathroom before turning on the other light.

Considerate.

She's not like her father. She'd never think about you the way he does. She doesn't treat other people the way he does.

Shame and confusion swirl in my head, and I don't know how I'm going to pretend to sleep tonight.

The bathroom door opens, the light off, and she slips under the covers, Sherman tucked between us. She lays down without jostling the mattress and sighs. "Caleb?" Her voice is quiet and sad.

"Yeah." I turn my head to look toward her in the dark.

"I'm sorry."

She's not like him.

I can't help but ask. "You okay?"

A rueful chuckle comes from her side. "No."

I HAVEN'T SLEPT for the last two nights. My brain's been a whirlwind of anxieties and old traumas, and my back's killing me. Tossing and turning have a tendency to make all my old hurts flare up.

I'm worn down and exhausted, and maybe that's why I finally agreed to go down for a group meeting. When I called Dr. Black and asked him if he had time to talk, it was his only condition. Despite the doctor-patient relationship, we've become something like friends. He also left the military after an injury, and I started using him as a sounding board from time to time. It's either the fact that I need to talk to him or because it's in the middle of the day and one more way to avoid Monica, but I agree. The prospect of three hours without her within ten feet of me feels like a reward for good behavior.

Whatever closeness we shared on Wednesday is blocked off from my thoughts. I can't be around her. Not when I'm not in control of myself. I know my aloofness has pissed her off, even if she's putting on a good show of giving me space. She knows, or at least is getting good at guessing, when to push and when to back off.

It's a dick move, but I take off without telling her. She

was at the lighthouse, climbing the stairs or working out of the second floor, I'm not sure which since I haven't been talking to her very much. Either way, she has to have seen the truck pull out.

My feelings for Monica are so distracting that I'm not even nervous about this meeting. When I get to the building where it's held, I'm surprised that the parking area is almost full. There are at least twenty cars here, and I spot Dr. Black's big white truck toward the far end. I park next to it and make my way inside without haste. In my rush to get away from home, I left way too early, and now there are almost twenty minutes before the meeting's supposed to start.

People gather around a table where coffee, water, and snacks are set up. Avoiding the gathering, I make a beeline for the opposite side of the room, wanting to avoid small talk as much as possible. I've never been great with crowds. I was a pretty shy kid growing up. After I got hurt, I avoided people even more since I never knew what to say and felt like I was always just trying to act normal.

I grab a chair and sit, pulling out my phone and ignoring everyone else around me. Just before the meeting gets underway, Dr. Black comes over and sits next to me. He knows me well enough by now that he keeps his mouth shut. He just nods when I glance at him, and I nod in return.

The meeting starts, and there's some general business in the beginning, a few readings, and then people get up one by one and start talking. They talk about how they've been doing since the last meeting, what they've struggled with, and what's been good. I don't realize when it was happening, but as each person spoke, I relaxed more and more and even started looking around the room and noticing how many people had things in common.

Even me.

Something unravels inside of me, realizing that so many of us have similar struggles even though we come from all different backgrounds and range in age from twenty to seventy, as far as I can guess.

The hour passes quickly, and when they announce the conclusion of the meeting, I blink in surprise.

"Let's wait until everyone leaves and meet in the lobby area for a little while," Dr. Black says.

I nod in agreement.

People filter out, some lingering for more coffee and some just catching up with friends. It's strange to watch groups of people who clearly didn't serve with each other but who are now friends. I haven't seen my unit since the accident, and that loss has left an ache in me that I haven't been able to name until now.

The last people leave, and only a handful of volunteers are left to help clean everything up. Dr. Black and I stand and move to another room, taking a pair of chairs farthest away from the door.

"Dare I guess this has something to do with your houseguest?" he asks with just a hint of a twinkle in his eye.

I snort. "Of course. But not just that."

He sobers and waits for me to continue.

"We were having a great night a few days ago."

He gives me a speculative look and raises his eyebrow suggestively.

"And then her father called."

"Ah." He nods and settles into his chair, lacing his fingers together and resting them on his stomach.

"I keep telling myself she's not like him, but then it seems like it keeps getting thrown back in my face that she's his daughter." It's like Ebenezer Scrooge dealing with all his Christmas ghosts.

"Do you want her to be like him?"

No. I want them to be so different that there's no resemblance at all. "Are you trying to be my psychologist now, too?"

He laughs, throwing his head back in a carefree expression of joy. "I prefer more physical problems. They're easier to diagnose."

"Like you don't enjoy a challenge." I smirk.

"Please. We all do. You want me to be honest with you?"

I nod since that's why I come to him instead of my therapist.

"I think you're trying to find ways that they're alike because she scares you."

"Please." I scowl, not wanting to let on how true it is.

Dr. Black just raises an eyebrow and waits.

"Alright, fine. But to be fair, I told her that."

"Really?" That seems to surprise him.

"Not in so many words. But yes, at dinner the other night."

He makes a sound of approval. "If you want my frank opinion, which you do when you call me out of the blue, this sounds like a risk worth taking. I don't know her, but I feel like I know you. If she's bothering you this much, you've got some serious feelings for her, and that's something you don't want to pass up."

"You're probably right." I sigh and stand. There's not much use in trying to avoid this any longer. "Thanks, man."

"Anytime. And do your PT exercises so I don't have to

bug your emergency contact again." He mock glares before we say goodbye and head out to our trucks.

THE STUPID FURNACE part is in the mailbox when I get back.

Just when I've started to come around to accepting the fact that I want to see if this thing between us can go anywhere, the universe sends the damn thing that will allow her to move back into the guest house.

Maybe I shouldn't say anything. I'll need Matt's help to install it anyway, and that will take a day or two. That would at least give me some time to sort things out with Monica.

I grab the box and shove it into the back of my truck. Of course, I'm going to tell her. There are enough things unsaid between us as it is. When I park the truck next to the cabin and get out, I look around as if I expect her to spring from behind a bush and call me out on disappearing all afternoon.

She's more likely to be in the house commiserating with Sherman about all the ways I'm a terrible human.

I head inside, and instead of being greeted by an angry woman, I smell something delicious cooking. The soft sounds of her singing emanate from the kitchen, and I can just make out the radio playing nineties country songs. Sherman is giving me the stink eye from the back of the couch, so at least something is normal about this surreal experience.

Quietly, I toe off my boots and hang up my coat, making my way toward the kitchen to face the music. Both literally and figuratively.

I stop in the doorway, taking in the sight of Monica

rocking fluffy socks, one of my flannel shirts wrapped around her, and her hair in a messy bun. It'' the least put together I've ever seen her, and she still looks stunning.

"You're back. I wasn't sure if you'd be home in time for dinner, but I made extra just in case." She glances over her shoulder with a smile, and I'm struck dumb by her calling my place "home" and the easy way she's accepting my erratic behavior. "Are you hungry?"

"Yeah." I'm an idiot.

"About ten minutes? Noodles just went in."

All I can do is nod, and she seems to accept that since she turns back to the stove and starts adjusting the knobs. At a loss for something normal to say, I turn around and flee to my bedroom, changing into a pair of sweats and a T-shirt.

It occurs to me that I should have brought her flowers or chocolates or some other gift to apologize for being an ass. She likely would have rejected all that anyway, preferring an honest explanation or, at the very least, a sincere apology.

Sherman strolls in and gives me a flick of his tail before jumping onto the bed and curling up in the sweatshirt I just threw there. "Thanks for keeping it real, dude."

"Can you get the dishes out?" Monica calls from the kitchen.

Glad to have something to do, I leave Sherman to his snoozing and go back into the kitchen, casting a wary look at Monica and then doing as she asked. Compelled by some urge to make things look nice, I grab placemats and put those down, too, along with a scented candle.

"This looks so pretty." Monica smiles as she brings a pair of ice teas over and sets them down. "Special occasion?"

"I'm sorry," I blurt it out. "About today, I mean. I should have told you where I was going."

She studies me, no doubt taking in how uncomfortable I am in my own skin at the moment. “You don’t have to apologize. You warned me you’d react badly to things sometimes. I figured this was just one of those.”

“Yeah.” I motion toward the stove. “Want me to dish it up?”

“Yes, please. Garlic bread is in the oven.”

I leave the music on low and dish up ample amounts of spaghetti onto both of our plates, stealing an extra piece of garlic bread for myself before carrying them over and setting hers in front of her. “Thanks for this.”

She smiles and digs in as soon as I put my plate down. Pausing, I watch her for a second. This feels so comfortable, so right, and I don’t want to act like an ass all the time anymore. “I really am sorry about today.”

“It’s alright.” Her words are mumbled around a mouthful of noodles.

Might as well dive right in. “I went to a veteran” support meeting in Sturgeon Bay.”

She must sense how much of a big deal this is for me to talk about because she sets her fork down and waits for me to keep talking.

“My doctor’s been after me for a while now to go to one. He’s been leading this one for veterans for years. I needed to talk to him, so we met up there.”

She studies me, face neutral. “You haven’t been to one before?”

“No.”

“You doing okay? Those can be pretty heavy.”

God help me; it would be so easy to fall in love with this woman. “I think so.”

"If you want to talk about it, just let me know. Otherwise, I won't bring it up again." Her smile is soft and accepting.

I nod, swirling my fork through the spaghetti. "Appreciate it." We eat in silence for a few minutes while I try to come up with some sort of small talk. "This is fantastic."

"Thanks. I asked Grandma to send me the recipe." Her delicate nibbles on the garlic bread make me feel loutish when I stuff a quarter of a piece in my mouth at a time.

"The part for the heater came today." Her eyes widen, and my heart lifts when I catch her faint frown. "I'll have to get Matt to come over and help me install it, so it might be a few days yet before I can get it up and running."

"Okay." She doesn't seem excited, and hope swells within me.

12

MONICA

The first thing I do when Caleb goes in the bathroom to get ready for bed that night is send Nore a message, asking her to stall Matt for a few extra days if Caleb calls him for help. I don't want to move back into the guest house. Caleb's cabin is cozy, he's got an adorable cat, and I'm enjoying our time together.

OOOO! You'll have to tell us all the details the next time we have a girls' night.

Caleb and I never told anyone about hooking up in the spring, and as far as she knows, I'm sleeping on his couch, so she's jumping to some pretty big conclusions there.

I have no idea what you're talking about.

I'm definitely not going to tell her something when I don't even know where things stand between us. Despite my initial irritation at his sudden disappearance today, I went with my gut feeling and trusted him to open up when he was ready. One thing I've figured out is the more you push him to do something you want him to, the more he'll resist.

My patience paid off. When I turned and saw him

lingering in the doorway, he looked tortured. For a split second, I was sure he was going to tell me I needed to leave. But he hadn't, and then when I didn't confront him, he'd seemed genuinely confused. Almost as if he expected me to snap at him.

Which I would have if I hadn't gotten to know him better these last few weeks. It makes me wonder about why he ghosted me this spring and turned into such an asshole. Was it something I did, or something he thought I did? I'm desperate to ask him about it, but if I come at him full force with questions, I know he'll shut down, and we'll take giant steps backward.

Patience, Monica.

I've just finished changing into pajamas when Caleb steps into the room, hesitating. Sherman's been snoozing on the bed, so I'm not sure what's making him linger on the far side of the mattress. In an unspoken agreement, we both pull back the comforter and get into our respective sides of the bed, leaving the neutral middle ground for Sherman to stretch out in.

I don't know why, but Caleb always shoves the comforter and sheets as far away as possible, but that also means I don't have to worry about him getting mad when I roll myself up in them throughout the night.

Caleb turns off the light and plunges the room into darkness. I'm not tired, so I settle on my back and look upward, letting my mind puzzle over things. It all circles back to wanting more time to figure things out with Caleb. I feel like, to do that, being here with him is essential.

"Do you think maybe we could try fixing the furnace together?" I ask, not sure if he's awake or asleep.

"We could." He pauses. "Matt's the one that fixed the

other one for me, but I watched him. I have a better idea of what to do now."

"If we had to, we could always call, but don't you think it would be fun to try first?"

He snorts, and I picture his slow smile. "Only you would think fixing an old furnace is fun."

"Can I ask a dumb question?" When he doesn't say no, I ask, "How come you don't just get new ones?"

This time he sighs, and I regret asking. On instinct, I brace myself for a biting, sarcastic response. "To be honest, I can't afford it. I'm stretching my budget pretty thin this year, and replacing two furnaces is not in that plan."

Shit. I know start-ups are risky, and I wonder how much of his own money he's used for this project. Just buying the property alone had to be expensive. Then doing all the restorations on top of it. If he didn't spend much of his salary when he was in the Army, he's going to be cutting things pretty thin, and I know he doesn't have a partner. He's probably got bank loans he'll need to pay down right away.

"Is that why you seemed so excited about the extended stay when I called?"

He shifts, rolling more to face me. "Yeah."

"You know I almost went to stay with Grandma just so I'd have someone to talk to? Then Nore, Sarah, and Andrea ganged up on me and told me I should talk to you."

Sherman resettles himself with a disgruntled huff.

"What did you wind up telling her you're doing?"

"Volunteer vacation. I feel bad lying to her, and I think she suspects something, but I just don't want to deal with Dad right now."

Caleb makes some sound of scoffing agreement. "I know that feeling."

I almost ask him what he means, but I figure I've stuck my foot in it too much already tonight. We lapse into silence, and before long, I hear the even sounds of his breathing along with the soft snore from Sherman.

"DID you never have to hold a flashlight for your dad?" Caleb grouches. We're both peering into the bowels of the furnace, and while the basement is well-lit, the furnace itself is large, and the part we're trying to replace is on the bottom in the farthest corner.

"You're joking, right?"

He flinches like I hit him. "Sorry. Sometimes I forget you guys aren't normal."

Although I think he meant it as some sort of apology, it sticks in my brain like a burr. He's been doing a good job looking past it lately, but I know he thinks I'm spoiled and never struggled. "Is anyone normal?"

"Probably not." He squats down, and I mirror his position, trying to hold the flashlight steady so it's not bouncing around like we're at a disco. We work in near silence for the next fifteen minutes. The only things he grunts are requests for me to hand him tools and, eventually, the part. I'm letting him do this all himself and just watching since messing with wiring makes me nervous.

"That should be it. You want to do the honors?" He points toward the switch on the side.

I don't, not really. If it's fixed, that means I have no more reason to stay in the cabin. I've gotten away with stalling for three days, but I ran out of excuses to keep putting it off this morning.

When the switch is flipped on, we both stare at the furnace, waiting to see if it turns on. To my disappointment, it gives a clunk and then hums steadily. Caleb seems satisfied and puts the cover back on before standing up.

"It might not be until tomorrow until it's comfortably warm in here again." Caleb looks over at me, and I can't tell if the regret on his face is because I can't move back in right away or that I won't be staying with him after tonight. "I don't want to turn it up too high and stress it out."

Nodding seems like the appropriate response, so that's what I do.

Then, an idea comes to me. If this is the last night I'll be staying with him, maybe I can make it special. Cook his favorite food and get him to watch a movie with me. Kind of like a stay-in date.

Feeling better now that I have a plan, I help him clean up the tools and follow him back upstairs. "What are you up to for the rest of the day?" I ask while we put our coats and boots back on.

"Ah." He hesitates, looking a shade uncomfortable. "I have to go to physical therapy this afternoon."

I knew he was still doing the exercises, but I didn't realize he was still going in for appointments, too. "Oh. Okay." That works out well since it'll give me time to get the surprise together.

We walk back to the cabin, and he glances at his watch, grimacing. "I've got to go soon, or I'll be late."

"It's alright. When will you be back?"

"Probably not until dinnertime."

"You need some food to take with? A sandwich, maybe?"

He's shaking his head before I even finish talking. "It's alright. I'll grab some drive-through."

I wait, watching him leave. Sherman peers at him from his position on the back of the couch. "Well, buddy. We've got a surprise to plan."

"Whoa."

"Surprise." Caleb holds up a small bouquet. It seems like we were both on the same wavelength about making tonight special.

"Thank you." I take them and inhale their light scent. They're not roses, so the aroma isn't overpowering. Each flower is a different color, vibrant splashes in what's otherwise a very masculine color scheme. "They're beautiful. I've got a surprise for you, too."

Sherman howls from between our feet. "You too?" He bends down and scoops up the big cat, cuddling him like a baby.

"He's a good supervisor. Let me put these in a vase."

His face looks blank for a second before a sheepish grin spreads across it. "Ah, I'm not sure that I own one."

"Large glass?"

He nods, and we both head toward the kitchen. "Do I smell pizza?"

"I thought since you have so much pizza in the freezer, you wouldn't mind that for supper? Maybe with a movie?"

"That sounds great." He reaches up to get the biggest glass he can find, and I notice he's moving with more ease than usual. The therapy session must have helped.

We work together to put the flowers in water and find all the things we need to enjoy pizza on the couch—mostly napkins and a couple of bottles of beer. I've already got the first Halloween movie pulled up, a subtle jibe at our last big fight. When Caleb notices the opening credits, he smiles and hands me a piece of pizza.

After we finish eating, I grab a blanket, cuddling close against his side. I duck my head against his chest at the scary parts. Horror movies have never been my favorite, but when I asked Andrea what I should pick, she said the genre would give me plenty of opportunities to "get close" to whoever. Several winking emojis surrounded it, so I'm pretty sure she also suspected what I had planned for tonight.

Caleb's arm settles around my shoulders, and his fingers play idly with my hair while he watches the movie. That he's not squirming nearly as much as I am makes me think he's enjoying it.

This feels good. Somehow, it makes me feel whole in a way I haven't found in a long time.

By the time the credits roll, I'm half in his lap, my head resting against his shoulder. "Thank you," he murmurs, pressing a kiss to the top of my head. It might just be my wishful thinking again, but it sounds like he's saying thank you for more than just tonight.

"You're welcome."

He shifts, and I sit up, leaving my legs across his lap when he keeps a firm hand on my thigh. "I mean it. Thank you."

"For what?" It's hard to breathe, my heart pounding against my lungs and my throat constricting.

"For not being the person I thought you were. For proving me wrong and calling me out on my shit all the time."

"Well, that's my pleasure." I grin, poking him in the ribs. "But who did you think I was going to be like?"

He shakes his head. "It's not important."

I think it is, but I'm still practicing this being patient thing and reminding myself not to push too hard. "Well, thank you too. You don't know how much this has meant to me. Especially you letting me stay here with you."

His hand traces looping patterns against my leg, and I try to scoot closer without being obvious. He watches me, more at peace than I've seen him in months. Slowly, reverently, he leans down, and our lips meet in a slow brush. "I know I'm not good enough for you," he whispers before deepening the kiss, sneaking his tongue out to brush along my lips and encouraging me to open up for him.

But I pull back. "What do you mean you're not good enough?"

His fingers flex in my hair as if he'd rather pull me back to him than answer the question. "I'm damaged goods, physically and mentally. Compared to you—" His eyes shift down, looking both at me and through me at the same time. "We're on different levels. You've got a degree and a 401k."

"That doesn't matter. None of it matters." I don't know how to make him believe that. Maybe my belief in him will be enough for now.

"See, the thing is, I think you believe that."

"Because it's true." I'm getting irritated with him, and the words come out sharper than I intended.

His eyes are dark and serious, but he doesn't deny it. Instead, he takes his hand from my thigh and brushes a few stray strands of hair from my face. "You're still too good for me."

"I don't want to argue with you about this." I glare at him. "Just shut up and keep kissing me."

He grins, boyish and far less serious than he was a

moment ago. "That's what you want, huh?" I nod vehemently. "Alright, princess. I can do that, at least."

This time, it's still slow, almost languorous, but deeper. So much deeper that I fight the urge to crawl all the way onto his lap and straddle him. His thumb brushes back and forth across my cheekbone as he cradles my face in his big hands.

God, this man. How can he think he's not good enough for me when this has been all that I've wanted?

It could be minutes or hours later when we break apart, with heavy breathing and languid bodies. "What if I told you I didn't want to move back into the guest house tomorrow?" I have to know what he's thinking.

"I'd say I don't want you to go either." I'm about to say I won't when he cuts me off. "But if we're going to give this any more of a go, then I think we need our own spaces."

"Moving in together is probably a red flag after one date." I try to smile at my joke, but it's forced.

"We have done things a little out of order." He shifts, and I finally take my legs off of him. He stands and helps me up. "I don't want proximity to cloud your judgment."

Patience, Monica. Be patient with him.

"What about just for tonight?" Please, God, don't say no.

"You're sure?"

Why is he so uncertain of himself? I feel like every time I figure a piece of him out, there's another, smaller knot I need to untangle. "Yes."

He takes my hand and pulls me along with him to the bedroom. Sherman must sense what's going on tonight because he's not curled up on the bed, and I haven't seen any sign of him since the movie started.

Caleb steps close, and I loop my arms around his shoulders. His hands settle on my hips, and I'm thankful we're about the same height, so I don't have to strain on my tiptoes. He pauses, but I'm sick of waiting. Sick of not taking what I want. I lean in and kiss him, using my grip on his shoulders to hold myself steady.

A deep noise of satisfaction rumbles in his chest, and his hands move, sliding around to cup my ass, squeezing and massaging, nudging me closer until one of his thighs wedges between mine.

"Caleb," I moan. "Bed. Please."

Obediently, he turns us, and we fall to the bed together. He lets me go long enough to scoot up more toward the middle, and he crawls over me. This is so different from that first time when we were both buzzed and in a rush. This feels more like a slow awakening or a long-awaited homecoming.

The way Caleb watches me makes me believe he's absorbing my every reaction. I widen my knees, and he lowers himself in between, bracing on his elbows and rekindling the slow kisses that started on the couch.

There's no trace of hurry in his movements, and I relax, following his lead and letting go of my usual need for control. My hands trace down his sides, slipping under the hem of his T-shirt and tracing along the skin at his waist. He shivers when I hit a ticklish spot. I make a mental note but don't pull away, unwilling to break our connection.

Slowly, so slowly, he shifts, and one of his hands brushes along the outside of my arm, tracing the delicate veins of my wrist and interlacing our fingers. He lifts, raising our joined hands to rest near my head. On instinct, I bend my knee, arching into him and pressing our bodies together.

"You're making this very difficult," Caleb grinds out,

pressing his hips into mine so I can feel his erection through his jeans.

"Well, something is certainly hard." There's a silent pause, and we both burst into laughter, Caleb collapsing on top of me.

"I can't believe you just said that." His breath fans against my neck, and I can feel his laughter reverberating in his chest. While he's relaxed, I lever up and rotate our bodies so that I can straddle him, admiring the way his tight T-shirt highlights his shoulder muscles. Our fingers are still tangled together, and he brings them up to rest over his heart.

The look in his eyes is tender and full of longing, but his face turns serious. I look down at him, staying still and waiting to see where he wants to take this.

"Can I take your shirt off?" He waits until I nod before sitting up, pushing me further back on my haunches. Like this, with us both sitting, we're eye to eye. He watches me watch him while his fingers slip under the hem of my shirt and inches it upward. I lift my arms, and his fingers ghost over them as he raises the fabric up and off.

Since I was hoping this might happen tonight, I put on one of the fancier sets of bra and panties that I brought with me and am rewarded with the widening of his eyes. His breathing speeds up, and I feel his thighs tense underneath me. "Yours too?"

He doesn't react for a minute, and then his eyes refocus, and he nods. I'm surprised at how much my fingers tremble as I slide them underneath his shirt, letting my palms rest against his abs and then smoothing upward until I can get the shirt all the way off.

Once his arms are free, Caleb settles his hands at my

waist, holding me steady as he dives back in for more kissing. We make out like teenagers. Each tease and brush of his skin, hair, and breath only raises my awareness to new heights.

At some point, he unbuttoned my jeans and slid his hands inside the waistband, massaging and kneading my butt, starting the slow roll of our bodies together that mimics what I hope we'll be doing at some point soon. The sooner, the better.

"Caleb," I gasp between breaths. "I think it's time to take our pants off now."

"Agreed." His voice has gone low and growly.

My legs are wobbly when I try to lever up and wind up just rolling off to the side, swinging to the side of the bed and turning my back to Caleb so I have a moment to steady myself. I can hear the bed moving behind me and then the thunk of his pants as they hit the floor. The sharp crackle of the condom wrapper makes me jittery with nerves.

I shift to the side, working one leg out of my pants and then the other. Then, unmoored and lost in the lust that Caleb's laced through my veins, I sit there, unsure of what to do. He comes around to my side of the bed, and my eyes track over the muscles of his thighs, noticing the tracings of old scars spreading up and disappearing into the leg of his boxers.

The first time we were together, the lights were off, and I was too lost in the moment to pay much attention. I never realized how significant his injuries were. He must see me looking at them and stiffens. I reach out, letting my fingers skate over the faintest of the marks, feeling the toughened layers of skin underneath.

"It's worse on my back." His voice is strained.

"Can I see?"

Without words, he rotates. I hold back a shocked breath. Deep red scars slash across his lower back, passing over his spine and fanning outward. I keep touching them, letting my fingers follow the lines of scar tissue. While I explore, he holds himself still.

"Does it still hurt?" I whisper.

"Sometimes."

I remember the way his back tightened up after he fell and can only imagine the pain he was in and trying so hard to hide. "The guys don't know about this, do they?"

"No."

"Caleb?" He half turns, glancing at me, and then away. "Do you like me touching you here?" I lay my palm over the worst of his scars.

"You—" He swallows deeply. "You don't mind them?"

I mind that he has them and want to ask what happened, but now is not the time. "No."

He turns again, and my hand rests at his hip, fingers slipping under the waistband of his underwear. "It feels...different. Not bad, but I'm not used to it either."

"Tell me if you want me to stop." I push lower, following a line of scar tissue and taking the boxers down with it. He steps out when they drop to his ankles, and I take a moment to brush my hands over his injuries, noticing how he's relaxing. I wonder if he's let anyone but his doctors see them this close before.

13

CALEB

This is happening. It's really happening. When I finished PT today, all I could think about was Monica and that she wouldn't be in my bed after tonight. Wouldn't share my space. I can't shake the feeling that she's slipping through my fingers.

On the way home, I got the idea to surprise her with flowers and then a proper date, so I stopped by a grocery store and picked out the most colorful bouquet they had. Coming home, I found that she had pizza and a movie ready. Everything spun out from that point, and all thoughts of a date left my mind.

Now she's touching me, not shying away from the scars or flinching at the worst ones that are still an angry red. The way she's embracing them, more than anything, is proof that she's not like her father, superficial and easily disgusted.

My attention lasers in when her delicate fingers brush against my painfully stiff erection, wrapping around the base and pumping upward. I can feel her panting breaths, and I might be imagining it, but I think I can hear her heartbeat, too. Her focused gaze is locked in on her hand, eyes unblinking with rapt attention.

On instinct, I gather her hair into a fist, praying that we're both on the same page here. Thank fuck she leans forward, her lips brushing against the head of my cock and sending shockwaves of sensation rocketing up my spine. Her tongue laps out, tasting the beads of pre-cum that have been leaking from me for the last hour at least, then trailing lower until she meets the tight fist of her hand.

Each breath she takes feels like an electric shock, a live wire connecting us. I watch as she licks back up and then, without a second thought, sucks my crown into her mouth. A broken, guttural moan fills the room, and it takes a moment to realize it came from me.

Her fingers flex around me, and she brings her other hand to my hip, steadying herself as she draws up and down, slowly at first, until she finds her tempo and gains confidence.

My toes tingle, muscles going taught, and I yank her head off before I come down her throat. Her lips are swollen, the bottom one jutting out in a way that makes me want to do whatever she wants. Plus, my pull on her hair bends her head backward, making her look like a pouting princess.

My princess.

Possession rages through me, and I ease her backward onto the bed, grabbing the condom from the side table where I threw it earlier. This woman is a drug that's breaking through all of my carefully constructed barriers.

The thought of her leaving bruises my heart. It makes me want to scream at the injustice of it and the feeling of loneliness that's already trying to crawl back in.

It's just like what I was afraid of. She has the singular power to ruin me. This little woman can break me to pieces when I haven't let anything else put more than a dent in my armor. I need her more than anything. I'd give up this property if she asked. Follow her anywhere if she wants me to.

Her leg hooks around the back of mine, so neither one of us can get too far away from each other. Her dark swath of hair fans out across my sheets, and the smooth, perfect expanse of her skin makes me want to kiss and touch every inch. Especially where the black lace bra is hiding her from me.

"Take this off." I flick the elastic of the strap, and to my surprise, she does what I ask. While she presses upward, I lean back, fumbling with the condom packet until I can get it open and roll it on. I don't want to risk forgetting later.

The black lace goes flying past me when she tosses it to the floor, and my focus zeros in on her beautiful breasts. She's on her elbows, thrusting them forward in an explicit invitation I can't resist. I frame them in my hands, reminding myself to go slow and savor the moment. I don't want to rush.

I dip my head, sucking her left nipple into my mouth without hesitation and then letting it go with a pop. It's flushed a darker pink and is glistening with my saliva. I give the other one the same attention and then blow, watching them harden.

Monica's breathing is turning more and more ragged, and I grin wolfishly down at her. Pleased that I can affect her just as much as she torments me. I make my way further down, kissing along the curve of her ribs. She grabs my arm and, in a growl that sounds more feral than anything else, demands, "Don't you dare. I need you. Now."

Her nails dig into my skin until I move back up, hovering over her and staring into her eyes. My heart is pounding with sudden nerves, afraid to take this next step with her and turn our relationship into something even more serious.

Not burdened by the same hesitation, she reaches between us. I feel her fingers wrap around me once more, guiding me toward her entrance. She holds me there, waiting for me to push forward.

I start with an agonizingly slow pace, making sure she's ready before I pick up speed. Each thrust and retreat draws more sounds from her. I bask in the feeling of her fingers on my skin, our bodies pressing together.

It doesn't take long before I'm lost in her, absorbing each reaction, my mind blank of any thought except giving her as much pleasure as possible. She's clenching around me, and then, faster than I ever thought possible, she groans, arms and legs tightening around me, head thrown back against the mattress, lost as she slips over the edge. And then I'm gone, too, shudders of pleasure racing down my spine.

I collapse, our bodies sealed together with sweat and heat. My ego savors the press of our racing hearts and the breaths we're both trying to catch as we come down.

After a few minutes, I peel myself away and take care of the condom before grabbing a spare blanket and going back to her, wrapping myself around her and then the blanket around both of us. She clings to me, face buried against my chest, a satisfied smile on her lips.

Her breathing evens out, but I'm still wide awake, listening to her, memorizing the feel of her against me, and thinking of all the ways she's already ruined me.

"WHAT HAPPENED?" Her fingers splay across my scars. I rolled onto my stomach during the night, my arm still wrapped around her waist to keep her close.

I turn my head, watching her face as she looks at the ruined skin.

"You don't have to tell me. I'm sorry." She withdraws, getting ready to wrap those protective layers back around herself.

"It was an accident. A stupid fucking accident." I roll to my side, holding the hand she was touching me with and looking at her pale, unmarred skin. "I can't say a lot."

She frowns but doesn't push me any farther.

"It was supposed to be an easy photo op with a politician and their kid. The kid just enlisted, and they wanted coverage that they could share on the local news or something."

I press her hand to my chest, my heart far steadier than I thought it would be when I finally opened up about my injuries. "The kid was an idiot. The only reason he hadn't gotten arrested by that point was because of his father. It was going alright until he snuck away for a smoke. His father found him and started laying into him. The kid chucked the cigarette and tried to argue his way out of whatever his dad was threatening him with. Long story short, it was a dry summer. The butt landed by an open ammo bunker, and it spread faster than anyone could have expected. I dove on top of the father to cover him just as a box blew up. Caught it right in the back."

I can't tell her that her father was there, that he saw it all happen and was the one who organized the cover-up afterward. It's all part of the first NDA her family had me sign.

Bile and anger try to roil up, but I repeat my new mantra. *This is not her fault. She's not like him.*

"Oh my god," she whispers, eyes wide.

"I didn't realize how serious it was until I tried to stand up and my leg didn't work right."

I'd been sick with fear, knowing that a single moment had just changed the whole trajectory of my life. The next few months were a blur of surgeries and doctor's appointments and therapy.

"Some of the shrapnel got close to my spine. Luckily, not too close." My words trail off, and my eyes fall shut. The doctors called it a miracle, but all I could think about was how much of a tragedy it was.

"Doctor Black, the one I met with at the group meeting, was the one who did the surgery. He got me up and moving again and has been trying to keep the scar tissue down. As he says, the goal is to prevent any more nerve damage so I don't wind up with a cane."

"Nerve damage?" she asks, face scrunching with worry.

"Most days it feels okay. Then there are some when it feels like the worst case of sciatica you've ever experienced. Shooting pain down my leg and back. I've gotten it more under control now, as long as I stick with the plan and don't push things too hard."

"Oh, my god. Last night—" She looks horrified, but I can't help but laugh.

"That's not how you're going to wreck me, princess. Don't worry about that." Her face turns bright red, and I pull her down for a kiss, settling her into my side and hiking the blanket up higher. It's still dark, so there's no need to rush out of bed. No rush to move her back into the guest house.

"Promise you'll tell me if you're hurting?" she murmurs, hands tracing up and down my abs.

"I promise."

We lay there, tangled together in the dark, until we dozed back off.

I SET the last box down just inside the door, reluctant to go any farther inside. Monica looks just as forlorn as she slips her coat off and hangs it on the rack. It's dark, and we've barely left the bed all day. But I insisted she stay here tonight with the explanation that I need to get up in the morning right away and don't want to bother her. It's as flimsy an excuse as I could muster.

Really, it was that I wanted to lock her inside my cabin and never let her leave. We both needed some perspective after last night and again this morning. It was dusk when we finally started moving her things back over, and now darkness was crowding against the windows.

Even Sherman was reluctant to see her leave, staying perched on top of a pile of her clothes until I had to pick him up and move him, which earned me a derisive swat and tail flick. I'll probably find puke in my shoe when I get home.

"That should be everything." Her voice is shaky.

"Yeah."

She nods, looking around at all her things where we piled them in the entryway. "You sure you don't want to stay for supper? Or maybe go out somewhere?"

"I shouldn't." The denial rushes out before the words of acceptance can even become a seed in my mind. I know what will happen if I stay, and my head and heart can't handle it right now, even if putting distance between us feels like an acute form of torture.

She nods some more, like a life-size bobblehead. "Right then." Her fingers knot together, and I feel like the biggest jackass in the universe.

I step forward, closing the distance between us and sealing our lips together in a heated kiss. She clings to me, trying to hold on for just a second longer, but I tear away and rush out the door.

I'm the worst sort of fool. Why can't I just accept this risk and try to hold on to what I long for? What I think has been missing from my life for so long.

Needing something to do, I head for the office. Work might help keep thoughts of Monica at bay. I open up my emails, the accounting software, anything, but nothing works. All I can think about is Monica and all the things I'm not allowed to tell her but so desperately want to.

14

MONICA

Even though I moved back into the guest house, I still see Caleb every day. If I don't drop by on the pretext of bothering Sherman, he'll come over to see me, either wanting to play a game of chess or watch a movie. More often than not, we'll wind up tangled together. Now that we've acknowledged it and opened ourselves up to it, the draw between us feels even stronger.

But he still insists on not staying the night when he comes over. And it makes me feel like I'm intruding if I stay the night with him at the cabin. So inevitably, in the middle of the night, one of us will get up and leave to go back to our little corners of the property.

Things have been so good between us. We're communicating and connecting on a deeper level, but I still have that lingering feeling that it isn't quite perfect. Maybe that's a naïve wish. No relationship is perfect, but it itches at my need to figure things out.

When we aren't together, I'm stalling with the work

they're letting me do, trying to drag it out as long as possible so that I'll have something to distract myself with. The need to get back in the office is growing, and I sent Naia a message this morning, asking when they thought it would be a good time for me to return.

I'm toying with the idea of requesting a hybrid schedule. That would give me more flexibility in where I worked from, so if things progressed with Caleb like I hoped, I wouldn't have to be away all week.

If nothing else, these last two months have shown me that when I'm in the office full-time, I struggle to keep the rest of my life together. I hadn't realized how burned out I was until they forced me to take some time for myself and slow down.

It wasn't like I was hurting financially. I have a healthy trust fund and make good money as a lawyer. Since I own my apartment and don't have pets, my monthly expenses are minimal outside of bills and food.

Caleb isn't in the same situation, though. I'm still not sure how he's able to afford this place other than suspecting that he got some kind of accidental injury settlement when he was discharged. There has to be a grant or program he could apply to as a new business owner or retired veteran.

I'm certain he hasn't looked into any of them yet since he's been so overwhelmed with the day-to-day of business ownership. Needing something to do, I start researching. After a couple hours of digging, I have a short list of five grants that look like decent contenders.

Better to ask for forgiveness than permission. I email each one, outlining who I am and who the applicant would be, and request more information. I don't know how Caleb will react if anything comes of this, but I smile, glad to feel like I'm helping him in my own way.

The next morning, I eagerly open my email, crossing my fingers that someone responded to my inquiries. They haven't, but Naia has.

There's been some forward movement with Alana's case, so our workload is ramping up. Come back to the office any time. Maybe take the rest of the weekend and start Monday?

She gives me a few more details about other projects that I'll be taking over while the office shifts to focus on the big trial against Alana and the other members of the criminal organization. I squint, the words blurring. I could go back to work in three days. Back to my gray apartment and long nights and takeout and microwave meals.

I'll let you know for sure before then. Can we schedule a meeting for sometime next week? I'd like to talk about my work arrangements in a little more detail.

There. That gives me time to decide when to go back but won't let me chicken out asking to make a change. I don't want to say anything to Caleb until I know it's a possibility, so for now, I file the email and smile. Content that I'm taking proactive steps in my life that are my choice and for my well-being.

"Hi." I beam too wide, feeling guilty for spending my entire day working on things for him without asking. "What's that?" My eyes fall on the giant, red cardboard heart wrapped in cellophane and another colorful bundle of flowers.

"Happy Valentine's Day?" Caleb thrusts the gifts into my hands, and it takes me a hot minute to process what he's said.

"Is it Valentine's Day?" I honestly haven't been keeping track of the actual date, just the day of the week.

"As far as I remember." Caleb looks like he's holding back laughter. "Girls still like flowers and chocolate, right?"

"Oh, yes." I throw myself at him, wrapping my arms around his shoulders and knocking the box of chocolates against his back. I kiss him soundly. "Thank you."

"There's more." He nods toward his feet, where a cooler bag rests on the patio. I recognize it right away as Andrea's since she uses it all the time when she brings food over.

"You didn't!" I screech, jumping up and down and almost upsetting both of our balances.

"I have strict instructions on what to do, so you should let me in before she finds out I didn't follow them."

He barely has time to pick up the bag before I shove him through the door and slam it closed. Andrea's been blowing up the group chat for months, asking us to give her ideas for Valentine's Day specials. She's nervous because it's her first big holiday with the restaurant open.

"Which one did you pick?" I hurry after him as he makes his way toward the kitchen. We helped her narrow it down to two options—a traditional steak dinner or a more daring venison recipe.

"I was going to go with steak, but Steve thought the venison would travel better."

My grin turns from happy to thrilled. "That's the one I picked out! I'm so excited."

Caleb gazes at me for a moment, an indulgent fondness in his eyes. Then he sets to work getting out the pans and things he needs to finish cooking the meal. I'm torn between my desire to watch Caleb move around the kitchen and the need to go primp and dress up now that I know it's a holiday and he's gone through so much effort to make it special.

In the end, my fascination with watching him wins out. Besides, he's in his normal clothes, so it's not a big deal. "Want me to do anything?" I ask when he puts all the food on plates.

"There are some candles in there." He nods toward the cooler bag. "If you want to light them?"

God bless Andrea and Caleb for coming up with this.

Caleb puts the finishing touches on the food while I dress up the table, lighting the candles and arranging the flowers. In a vase this time. Apparently, there are some stashed away for welcome arrangements.

When he pulls out my chair and steals a quick kiss, my heart flutters in my chest, and excitement hums through me. The smell of food and wine fills the kitchen, and I couldn't have dreamed up something more perfectly romantic than this.

"The food looks just as good as when Andrea makes it." My mouth's watering.

"Do me a favor." He settles across from me at the table, and I raise an eyebrow. "Don't tell Andrea that. I value my life too much."

Laughter bubbles up, and I throw my head back, letting it flow through me. "I won't."

He nods, satisfied that I'll protect him from my best friend, and then fiddles with his phone until soft music spills from recessed speakers I hadn't even realized were there.

This man is setting the bar so high, there'll be no other

competition. The little voice in my head sobers me with that thought, and I gaze at Caleb, watching him as he cuts into the meat and takes a tentative bite. He might think I can ruin him, but he has just as much power over me.

"This is good." He glances up, noticing I haven't touched mine yet. "Don't worry, I followed her directions to a T."

"I'm not. I—" I just like watching you. Everything about you fascinates me. I think I might love you a bit too much for my well-being. With a forceful mental shake, I keep the words to myself. "Thank you. No one's done something like this for me in a very long time. Probably not since the year before Paul left for college, and he threw me a surprise birthday party."

Well, that's a mood killer, Price. Now he knows your family is shit, and you're a lonely hermit who works herself to the bone with no friends.

His eyes are serious and intense. "My pleasure."

We eat and make small talk. Between the two of us, we polish off a bottle of Cranbernet from Door Peninsula Winery, and I'm pleasantly tipsy by the time we clean up. After we finish, we stand side by side at the sink, him washing and rinsing and me drying and putting away.

The beat of the music sways through me. I move between the sink and the cupboards, letting myself sway to the subtle rhythms of the song, eyes half closed, still dressed in my sweats and oversized sweatshirt.

Big hands catch my hips as I move toward the sink, and my eyes drift open, gazing up into Caleb's intent expression. He looks hungry, lit from within, and it sparks the flame inside of me, too.

"You're so gorgeous," he murmurs, fingers flexing against

me, urging me closer. I allow myself to sway into him, letting our bodies press together and seizing the opportunity to slide my hands under his shirt and across his abs, the warm heat of him making me feel even more wanton and needy.

"Mmm. You too." My smile is lazy but satisfied.

He harrumphs a self-deprecating sound that makes me want to prove him wrong. I want to worship at his feet and show him how deserving of praise he is, but he must see the intent in my eyes because he scoops me up and sets me on the island counter before I can do anything. He cages me in with his body pressed between my legs and his powerful arms bracketed against the counter on either side of my hips. "None of that now. Tonight's all about you."

"That's not fair." I let myself whine, loving how his eyes spark and his body tenses. He crowds closer, leaning in until I'm forced to either push him away or lie back on the island.

I opt for lying back.

"Good girl." His grin is playful and eager, and his fingers are already working at the knot holding up my sweatpants. "I'm gonna take these off, and then you're gonna let me eat as much as I want."

My only answer is a shaky nod, adrenaline pounding through me. My brain snags at the wayward thought that I've never had sex in the kitchen before. A hysterical laugh almost escapes, but I clamp a hand over my mouth to hold it in.

"Uh-huh." Caleb shucks off my sweats and pulls my hand away. "I want to hear every single sound you make."

I'm going to melt into a puddle on the counter. I'm so turned on right now. *Oh god, what if I leave a puddle on the counter?*

All my irrational worries vanish when Caleb's calloused

fingers pull my thighs further apart and yank my hips closer to the edge of the island. Worry flashes through me. "Caleb. Don't kneel on the floor. We can go to the bedroom or the couch or something." I'll feel horrible if he hurts himself.

His smile is indulgent, pleased with me for some reason that I can't figure out. "I've got a chair. Try to relax."

"Oh." I flop back against the counter, but some of the frenetic energy has dissipated. It feels more serious now, somehow more real.

The beat of the music quickens with a new song, and Caleb sits, scooting closer until he can trace over my panties with one finger, then two, moisture already staining the fabric. Thankfully, my fingertips just reach the edge of the counter, and I latch on, holding on for dear life.

I'm panting, the cool marble making my skin even more sensitive. Self-consciousness makes me notice every place he touches me, whether with fingers, a breath of air, or the brush of his shoulders against my calves.

"I think." He stands a little, hands tracing up the crease of my thigh, pushing the elastic of my underwear up and up until it's stretched almost to my waist. It must be barely covering me, and the thought of baring myself to him makes me feel wanton. Sexy in a way only Caleb's been able to bring out. "You're still too covered up."

He shoves my sweatshirt upward, keeping my arms in the sleeves but bunching the rest just above my heaving chest. It creates a thick wall that blocks my view of what he's doing, and I moan, excited at the idea of letting him do whatever he wants without being able to see what's coming next.

"Jesus Christ. Have you not had a bra on all night?"

"They're uncomfortable." I lift my head up, peeking

enough to see him. He's made no secret of his fondness for my body, but my boobs have been a particular favorite of his.

"Christ." He mutters something else I can't catch, and then his fingers are plucking, cupping, massaging my chest until I'm sure my skin is rosy from his attention. Sweat gathers along my sternum and the crook of my spine, and I nudge the chair with my foot, trying to encourage him to sit down and get back to business.

Instead, he leans down, licking up the sweat and sucking hard on my nipples before nipping down the center of my body with stinging bites. I'm going to have a beard rash everywhere tomorrow, but I don't care.

"Caleb. Please." I thrust my hips upward, gyrating, so he'll focus back on where I need him most. This time, he takes the hint and his fingers find me, shoving my underwear to the side before sliding one in. He withdraws and adds another, working me higher while he settles himself on the chair. My head falls back, eyes staring up at the ceiling as stars of pleasure burst around me.

His fingers leave me, and I hear a sucking sound. He must have licked them clean, and I shudder at the delicious thought. Then his mouth is there, warm breath fanning across me before his tongue flicks out, nudging my clit and sending another shower of pleasure through me.

He's intent, methodical, working me up just to the edge of an orgasm and then slowing, changing his rhythm and angles so I'm not quite *there* but always hovering just on the edge of pleasure.

I'm never going to look at this island the same again after this.

Inarticulate sounds of pleasure fall from my lips in a

constant babble, and finally, finally, I lift my head, weak with pleasure, and make eye contact with him. I don't say anything, and he doesn't stop moving until I'm coming, pleasure flooding through me and blackness filling my vision.

15

CALEB

This might have been a colossal mistake, but it's one I know I'd choose over and over again. Feeling her come apart around me, knowing that even while she's lost in her own pleasure, she cares enough to stop and make sure I'm okay. It's all too much.

My feelings are battering at me, demanding to be let through so they can wrap her up in a cocoon of sweet warmth and caring. I've kept them locked away for too long, starving them in the barren corners of my heart.

I haven't let myself get too close, always keeping a superficial barrier between us. Whether it was to convince her that we needed the perspective of not living together or making sure I never spent the night, I made sure that distance was in place. I never let myself wake up next to her after a night of making love so that I wouldn't get used to what it felt like.

Fool. I berate myself, all while watching her, touching her, settling her from her high.

"Caleb." She listlessly lifts her head, eyes half closed and cheeks flushed red. "Take me to bed now?"

This is one time when I regret not being able to carry her. I'd love to scoop her up and cradle her close while I tuck her in, but my back is definitely not up for that. Instead, I help her sit and then get down from the counter, grabbing her discarded sweatpants and taking them with us.

The walk across the house wakes her up enough that by the time we reach the wide, queen-sized bed in the downstairs guest room, she's no longer content for me to just lead her.

This time, she takes control, pushing me down onto the mattress and climbing on top of me. Ravenous and greedy.

Stunning.

I barely have time to grab the condom out of my pocket before she's whipping my clothes off and returning every sensation I just teased from her body tenfold. With my last grip of self-control, I set her off of me and shove the condom on before guiding her hips back above mine and thrusting upward.

Mine. Mine. Mine.

Home.

We both fall apart, tangling ourselves in the sheets and a tossed-off blanket. Just before we drift off, her hand clings to mine, squeezing tight. "Don't leave tonight. Please stay." She sounds just as desperate as I feel. There's no way I can deny her.

"I'll stay." It settles her enough that she relaxes and lets herself drift off, still splayed across my chest.

I love you.

It drifts through my head, and I almost mouth the

words, wanting to see what they feel like. But I don't. They're still too dangerous for my heart, even if it's not any less true.

WHEN I WAKE up in the morning, she's right there. Tucked against me like we belong side by side, even in sleep. I still don't think I'm good enough for her, and I'm sure one day she'll realize that.

But now that I've tasted this feeling of wholeness, I don't want to live without it. She makes me feel again. To want to be a better person and keep healing because she believes I can. I want to keep trying to be someone she can show off to her fancy friends.

If I'm being honest with myself, that probably wouldn't even matter to her. It's just a reflection of how I think about myself. I've always felt like I wasn't good enough. My parents tried hard to make a good life for us. They were always busy, distracted by trying to make ends meet and keep a house over our heads. Compared with Matt and Steve's families, I felt like a charity kid visiting Disneyland whenever I went over to their places.

All that matters now is that I'm good enough for her to want to keep around.

She stirs against me, and I still, squeezing her closer to me and trying to seal us into this moment forever. Her fingers leave my chest and push her hair out of her face, eyes blinking open against the bright morning light. "You stayed." Her sunny smile is addictive.

"I stayed."

She tugs the sheet higher, tucking it around us more. "Do you have to do anything right away today?"

"No." I breathe in the scent of her, sweet and welcoming.

"You want to just hang out? Spend the day together?"

That sounds like paradise. I haven't taken a whole day off in months. "I'd love to."

She snuggles into the crook of my neck, looping her arm across my chest and throwing her leg over mine. "Can it start with a very lazy morning in bed?"

"Whatever you want to do today."

Her chuckle vibrates through me. "That's a dangerous offer."

"I trust you."

I can feel her lips tip up into a smile against my neck, and I hug her closer, helping her rotate so that she's more on top of me than on the bed. We stay like that for over an hour until the light from the sun is streaming through the window, and it's harder to ignore the ever-present hard-on I have whenever she's close by.

I shift, trying to be stealthy, and move it away from her, but she stirs, her leg rising and brushing against me. She freezes and then, with careful determination, reaches her hand out for me. We don't leave the bed for another hour.

Afterward, we cram together in the shower, washing up, touching, and savoring the connectedness that I'm trying to let myself be brave enough to hold on to.

"I have to go feed Sherman, but then do you maybe want to go on a snowmobile ride? Or a walk?" I ask, watching as she dries her hair and goes through her after-shower routine.

"Getting out of the house for a little while sounds wonderful. I don't know how you lasted through last winter."

Sometimes, neither do I. I was still hurting pretty badly,

and between the doctors' appointments and meetings with my therapist, it felt like I was always battling with something. "Sherman helps. He's quite a demanding boss."

She snorts and gives me a fond look. "I still can't believe you have a cat. Although looking back, he suits your personality."

I straighten up in mock affront. "Are you saying I'm demanding?"

Her cheeks flush, and her eyes flit down. "Sometimes, but I never said I didn't like it."

With intention, I stand up, prowling closer to back her up against the counter. That pretty flush is moving down her neck, and I know soon it'll spread across her collarbones. Her chest rises and falls with each rapid breath, and I lean close, not quite letting our lips touch. "You are a temptation that's extremely difficult to resist." I brush my lips across her cheek and down the side of her neck, easing her hair aside to expose her shoulder. It's bare since she's still only wearing a towel.

"Caleb." Half plea, half confused question.

I pull back, putting some distance between us so we won't get distracted again.

"Not fair," she pouts, still standing pressed against the counter, hands clenched over the edge.

"Get dressed. Wear something warm. It's sunny but still chilly." Needing a minute, I leave the bathroom, gathering my clothes and putting them on. I'll have to add a couple of layers when we get to my house, but for now, this works.

Within thirty minutes, we're out the door and heading to my cabin, walking side by side, holding hands. It all feels too perfect, and I can't shake the feeling that this perfect won't last. I shove those thoughts aside as I take care of Sherman.

There are trails through my woods, and my neighbors don't care if I ride on their property, so we could be out all day. I stuff some food and water in a bag in case we decide to.

When we approach the storage shed, Monica's steps slow, and she shoves her hands into her pockets as she eyes the sled. "You've never ridden on a snowmobile before, have you?"

She shakes her head. "Dad said they were too dangerous. Like motorcycles. It was one thing Mom agreed with him on. I don't think my brother has ever been on one either."

"You'll be safe with me. I've been driving one of these since I was a kid." I put the food and drinks in the bag I keep attached to the back and check that the gas tank is full.

She helps me drag it out and watches my every move as I turn it on. Before we get on, I go back to the shed and grab the helmets I keep stored there. They're both my size, but with all her hair, it should still fit her well enough. And she'll be warmer with it on. I already made her put on a pair of my thick winter gloves because I was worried about her hands getting cold.

Paranoid about her safety, I help her put the helmet on, double-checking the fit and securing it before sweeping my eyes over her outfit, reassuring myself that she'll be warm enough. I don't tell her any of this since I know she'd tell me she's fine and can take care of herself.

With a satisfied nod, I put my helmet on and throw a leg over the seat, motioning for her to climb on behind me. Like a natural, she slides onto the seat and puts her feet up. Her arms wrap around me, and I smile, anticipation filling me.

As soon as the sled moves forward, her arms clamp

around me, and her body goes tense. Not wanting to scare her, I take it easy on the throttle. The first part of the trails has already been tamped down from moving the four-wheeler around to pick up wood all winter, so we can keep it slow and smooth until she relaxes.

It takes almost half an hour of driving around in slow, looping circles before she settles against me and I go a little faster. When the speed picks up, she clamps herself around me again but eases up little by little.

I can feel her lift her head off my back, the hard edge of the helmet finally lifting away. The countryside is beautiful, and I hope she's enjoying the views. Up ahead, a wide field stretches out without a trace of humans on it. A few deer trails and some bird markings are all that mars the wide expanse of white. I ease back, slowing the sled so I can lift my visor and ask if she's okay with diving into it.

"How are you feeling?" I holler over the noise of the motor and the muffling of the helmet.

She grins through the visor and holds up a thumbs up. Her eyes are bright, and her cheeks are flushed with excitement.

"You okay going through the field? There isn't a trail, so there's going to be some powder; it might be a little less smooth."

She grins emphatically, and I smile back. "Make sure you hold on."

Knowing she's willing, I gun the throttle and go for it, savoring the speed and power of the snowmobile and the way she holds me tighter. When we hit the open field, the sled fishtails a little before getting traction back, and the engine revs as we plow through the snow.

She whoops in excitement, and I do spiraling circles

through the field, smiling under my helmet. Eventually, I steer us toward a clearing that looks out over the lake. It's not as good as the view from the lighthouse, but it's quiet and sheltered from the wind. We're also well into the afternoon, so she's probably hungry.

When she climbs off, her legs are shaky, and I hold her hand longer than I should. *It's just to keep her from stumbling.*

She fumbles with the straps of her helmet before eventually getting it off. "That was so much fun!" Her yell startles a few birds from a nearby tree, and they fly off, squawking.

"I'm glad you liked it." I take off my helmet, grab hers, and line them on the seat so they stay dry. "There're snacks and water in the cooler if you're hungry."

"You are the literal greatest."

I nod, keeping my face serious, and she swats my arm playfully. We stand at the edge of the cliff, watching the lake and snacking until she's ready to go again.

THE ENGINE SHUTS OFF, and I help Monica climb down. We stayed out all day, going into town after eating to get more gas and food and warm up a little before we tore around again. I even convinced her to try her hand at driving, but she insisted I take over so she wouldn't break it.

"Why don't you head in, and I'll put everything away?" I lean in and give her a quick kiss. Her cheeks are blazing red from the rubbing of the helmet and the cold.

"Thank you. I think I'm going to start a hot shower. I haven't been able to feel my toes in a while."

"Me either." We share a heated look, and then she steals another kiss before dashing through the back door. Before it closes, I hear her cheerful greeting to Sherman and the start of a one-sided, chattering conversation.

It takes ten minutes to put everything away and lock the shed back up. The only thing on my mind is joining her in the hot shower, but when I step through the backdoor, I hear her talking.

Except it's not to Sherman.

"You can't be serious." She sounds irritated, almost disbelieving. Must be a phone call.

"Can you even do that? She's got a laundry list of charges against her, and a majority of them are felonies." My heart sinks, dread filling me. I'm almost certain she's talking about her friend Alana.

"I can't believe that you're asking me to do this." Her voice has gone quiet, and she sounds beaten down. I want to step in and rip the phone out of her hand, but one word freezes me in my tracks. "Dad, if anyone found out—"

She's talking to her father. Her father, who it seems is trying to get her to do something that would either get her friend out of jail or get her charges reduced.

Her fucking father.

"I don't know right now. Give me some time to think, and we'll talk later."

Tell him no. Whatever he's planning, tell him no. That you won't do it.

But she doesn't say anything else. The only sound in the house is the shower running. She probably turned it on to get ready but got interrupted by his call.

"I'll either call you or we can meet up for lunch. I'll be back in town later this week." He must cut her off because she doesn't speak for a few moments.

"Well, I'm very fortunate the partners are so generous.

Naia's a wonderful mentor, and I've saved plenty of personal time. My vacation won't affect anything." He talks more and then must hang up on her if her slight startle and glare at the phone mean anything.

"Oh, hey. I didn't see you there." She sounds surprised, and I realize that I'm standing rooted in place in the kitchen doorway. Sherman's winding in between my legs, head-butting my shins, and making a soft and comforting, half-purring, half-rumbling sound.

I want to say something, anything, to untangle the sudden snarl of my thoughts.

"Shower should be plenty hot. I turned it on, and then my dad called." She holds up the phone, still gripped in her hand. She looks uncertain, cautious, like she's approaching an IED that's about to explode.

"What'd he want?" I'm proud of how normal that sounded, even to my ears.

Her lips purse, arms crossing across her chest. "He's trying to get me to do what he wants. Again."

I nod.

"Sometimes I wish I was more like my brother. He's so good at being able to minimize Dad's influence in his life." Her arms unfold, and she shakes off the conversation. "Are you joining me?"

Hopeful, a little shy, gorgeous.

Dangerous. The Prices are all dangerous.

"Go on ahead. I'll start supper."

Her posture sags with disappointment, but she doesn't argue, and I watch her disappear into my room. What I've started thinking of as our room. I listen to the bathroom door close and the slide of the shower curtain.

Whatever he was planning, she hadn't told him no.

And whatever her father was planning couldn't be good. Paul Price Senior doesn't deal in the currency of good deeds. He deals in the shadows, the subtle strings of power that keep him untouchable and well-liked. Favors that give him control of the future and what he needs in the present.

She can't be like her father. She'll tell him no.

But my gut tells me it's only a matter of time.

16

MONICA

The hot water streams over me, pulling out the cold that burrowed deep in my bones during our long day outside. Rage and disappointment war within me. Part of me still wants my dad to care about me and listen to what I want. Another part knows that he'll always put himself first and that I should have expected something like this.

I've been unreachable for too long. I might have gotten away with three weeks, but six? He had to bring me back to heel, and he chose this set of options: run for office, and he'd get Alana pardoned. If I positioned myself to be the district attorney in five years, he'd make sure her charges were reduced. My unspoken choice is to do neither, but that means he'll make sure she serves the maximum penalty.

Two impossible options that left me no choice at all.

I wish Caleb was here in the shower with me. He'd hold me and distract me from my shitty family.

I've been trying to savor what could be my last few days here. One thing was certain: I have to go back to my real life.

Sooner rather than later. And it's breaking my heart to even think about leaving Caleb for more than a day or so, especially after how well we've been doing.

Forcing myself to turn off the shower so there's hot water left for him, I step out and towel off, leaving a towel wrapped around my hair while I throw a pair of Caleb's sweatpants on and one of his long-sleeved shirts. Maybe I can convince him to let me stay over again tonight.

When I get closer to the kitchen, I walk carefully so I don't make a noise and sneak up behind Caleb, snaking my arms around his waist and laying my head against his back. He stiffens at my touch, and a bolt of unease tightens in my stomach. I loosen up in case I'm hurting his back. "Smells good. Want me to take over so you can shower?"

"Sure." He slips away from me without looking, and I'm stunned by the rejection. After basking in the warmth of his openness and affection all day, the cool bricks of his walls are an unforeseen surprise.

Maybe he's hurting and tired. Maybe he's got something on his mind. A shower will do him good. I'll have dinner ready when he gets out, and he'll feel better after he eats.

Only he doesn't, and all my plans to stay seem to evaporate into thin air.

Before it's even fully dark, I'm on my way back to the guest house, alone and confused.

Caleb's still acting distant two days later. He's been avoiding me and spending long hours holed up in his office.

I'm not stupid and can take a hint. So, I leave him alone, not even bothering to tell him I'll be going into the office this afternoon for my meeting with Naia. With the turn our relationship has taken, I'm not sure why I'm bothering to rearrange my life so I can spend more time with him.

Just give him time, and then you can talk about it like civilized adults.

My coat is hanging by the front door. I grab it, tugging it on with jerky motions, and throw my purse over my shoulder. I'll be surprised if he even notices I'm gone. Tears of frustration threaten to fall, but I sniff, shoving them back down and squaring my shoulders.

If there's one thing my father taught me well, it's how to put on a mask so no one will know what I'm thinking. Sometimes, I'm so good at wearing the mask that even I'm not sure what I'm feeling.

I turn on a podcast for the drive, something serious to distract me from thoughts of Caleb and my desire to barge in and shake some sense into him. My clock reads five to three by the time I pull into our parking lot at work, right on time.

Alicia greets me at the reception desk, throwing herself at me and giving me the tightest hug. "I've missed you so much," she half screeches with excitement.

"I've missed you too. Thank you for your help these last couple of months." She's been my primary contact with the office, sending me updates and files via email and the occasional phone call.

"Naia's in her office and ready to see you." We walk down the hall, past my office, and toward the one at the very end. "Does this mean you're coming back?" Alicia's face fills with hope.

"Yes, hopefully next week. I'll let you know all the details when we're done with our meeting."

"Can you stay for dinner?"

God, that sounds wonderful. "Sure."

She squeezes my hand before opening the door for me.

Naia stands from behind her desk and greets me with a hug, although it's not as chest-squeezing as Alicia's. "It's good to see you. You're looking well."

"Thank you. I hate to admit it, but the time away did me good."

She nods and motions for me to sit next to her in the pair of guest chairs. I get an eerie sense of déjà vu, as we're in almost the same positions as the day she told me I needed to take time off. "I'm hoping this meeting is to discuss your official return to work."

Here goes. "Yes. But I'd also like to discuss the possibility of moving to a hybrid schedule. I'd like some flexibility to choose which days of the week I'll be in the office."

We spend the next half hour discussing terms and going over a newly renegotiated employment contract I drafted and brought with me on the off chance she'd be open to my ideas.

Gathering up my courage, I bring up my next topic of conversation. "I also think my father is trying to interfere with Alana's case. I need your help to make sure that doesn't happen."

Naia, ever the calm and steady one, studies me with knowing eyes before nodding once and reaching for her phone. "Let me make a few calls. Can you stay longer?"

I nod, relieved that she's taking me seriously and ready to take action.

When I get back to the guest house, I'm surprised to see the lights still on in Caleb's cabin. It's almost eleven, and he's not much of a night owl. A brief tug at my heart pulls me toward him, but I resist. He never sent a text or tried to call while I was gone, and part of me needs him to be the first one to reach out this time.

I pull my car into the parking spot closest to the guest house's front door and get out, sighing in relief when I straighten. My back is stiff from the long drives back and forth, and my feet throb from wearing heels again. I can't wait to take off my dress and stow my shoes back in their box. I've gotten used to not wearing them, so the incessant pinching of my toes is more annoying than usual.

After I put everything away and go through my nighttime routine, I glance out the window. Caleb's lights are off. I check my phone, hoping to see a message. Even a simple goodnight would be better than deafening silence.

But there's no notification on my screen of an unread text or missed call.

And nothing the next morning.

Or afternoon.

Or evening.

I'm going over there. This is ridiculous.

It's dinner time, and I've already eaten, but I bet he hasn't. Needing some excuse to explain my appearance, I throw some leftovers on a plate and set out. I have three more days until I officially move back to Green Bay, and I feel like I need to tell him that in person.

I stomp across the yard and onto the narrow path that cuts through the edge of the woods. When Caleb's cabin comes into sight, I stop and square my shoulders, reminding myself that I'm doing the right thing in confronting him.

As I draw closer, my steps are purposeful and confident. With great restraint, I knock on the door politely, not the hammering I wish I could give it. The lights are on, so I know he's home, but I don't hear movement inside. I knock again and see the curtains move as Sherman pushes his way through the gap. The glass muffles his plaintive yowl, but I still hear it. "I know, buddy. Where's your dad?"

I circle around the back of the house, thinking he might be working in the shed or chopping more wood. My hunch pays off as I hear an axe connecting with wood. Rounding the corner, I come face to face with Caleb, covered in sweat, axe in hand, a hard expression on his face.

"How long have you been out here?" I ask, concerned that he might overdo it based on the way sweat plasters his shirt to his torso.

"Dunno."

"Have you eaten?"

He sets the axe down and pulls off his gloves. "No."

"Good, because I brought you leftovers." I hold out the plate like an offering, and he takes a tentative step forward. "And we need to talk."

His shoulders bunch up even higher, but he gives me a curt nod and lets me follow him into the house. He washes his hands, and I stick the plate in the microwave to warm it up.

"I'm getting ready to go back to Green Bay." Might as well get straight to the point. "I'll drive down Sunday afternoon, so that can be my checkout date."

He doesn't say anything. I take the plate out of the microwave and put it at his spot on the table. He stays by the sink, staring just past me, face expressionless.

"Is this one of those times where you're reacting badly to

something?" A hint of exasperation is creeping into my voice.

He nods, back stiff, and I see the careful way he's carrying himself.

"Sit down." I point toward the chair and glare until he listens. My patience is wearing thin, and I don't have it in me to be soft with him. I get an ice pack from the freezer and shove it in his hands. "Use it."

Obligingly, he puts it across his lower back. "Thanks."

"Do you want a painkiller, too?"

He shakes his head and scoops some food onto his fork but doesn't eat it. "Can I ask you a question?"

"Please do." I take the seat across from him, waiting to see what he'll say.

"If you knew someone was going to do something bad, something they'll regret, would you tell them? Or would you let them figure it out on their own?"

I pause, trying to riddle out what he's asking. "Is this about one of your friends from the military?"

"No." He shakes his head. "No, nothing like that. Just a friend who might be about to make a mistake at work."

Is this what's been stuck in his head? "It depends. But I'd lean toward letting them figure it out on their own. The only people I feel like I know well enough to talk to about their careers would be my assistant or one of the girls."

His lips purse, and he moves the food around on his plate. "Alright."

It looks as if he's come to some sort of conclusion, but I'm not sure it's good. My answer only seems to make him withdraw from me even further. "I already ate, so I'll go." Not wanting to cause a massive blow-up, I stand, pushing my chair back in. I wasn't even here long enough to need to take off my coat.

"Monica." Caleb's voice gives me a moment of hope.

I turn to face him. "Yeah?"

He looks at me, studying me like I do some of my clients. "You know you're one of the smartest women I know, right?"

My brow wrinkles in confusion. "Thanks?"

Caleb scrubs a hand across his face. "I mean, it's good that you're going back to work."

I watch him for a moment. "I'm looking forward to it, but I think I'm also ready to make some changes."

His eyes widen in dismay. "Really?"

"Yeah." I rub at the bridge of my nose. "Before I left, I was getting close to burnout. I'm sick of working ninety hours a week without a break."

"That's good." He clams up. "I mean, it's good that you're arranging things to suit you more."

I did it to spend more time with you, you dolt. But I keep that thought to myself. "Are we okay?" I have to know, or I won't stop worrying about it.

His eyes flick past me, not quite looking at me. "Yesterday, I thought you left."

Oh, Caleb. "I had a meeting, and I stayed for dinner with some friends from the office."

He nods, looking relieved but still closed off.

"I'll talk to you tomorrow?" I ask, needing some confirmation that he's going to stop avoiding me.

"Yeah." His smile is weak.

Without pressing him anymore, I walk out the door.

17

CALEB

My reflection in the mirror looks like the me of two years ago—haggard and hollow. I know I'm making a mistake in pushing her away, but I can't seem to stop myself. My therapist would tell me to talk to her and give her a tenth of the trust and loyalty I want in a relationship.

That upcoming lecture is why I haven't called to set up my next appointment yet.

I should go over there. She's leaving today, and I've still been avoiding her. Yesterday, I wandered over, not sure what to say, and we wound up playing a few silent matches of chess. When we finished, and she looked like she wanted to talk about something personal, I made a lame excuse and left.

She's pissed, and deservedly so. Even though I recognize that I'm acting like an ass, I can't help myself. I don't want her to leave or want this thing between us to end, but I also don't know how to get around my issues with her father.

Sherman stares at me from the top of his cat tree, tail

flicking back and forth in mocking swishes. His deathly, serious stare tracks every move I make. Looks like he's pissed at me, too.

The least I can do is help her pack her car up. The number of files she has is truly frightening. Shuffling them back out of the guest house seems like a good peace offering. Mind made up, I shove my feet into shoes and hurry over to the guest house.

I knock on the door, self-conscious about barging inside when I've made things between us weird. Over the last few weeks, we've taken to just coming and going. "Come in." I hear her holler. The protective instincts inside me want to chastise her for at least not checking who it is first.

But if I did that, I'm pretty sure she'd bite my head off.

"Hey." I step in and close the door so the heat won't escape. A bitter wind started blowing in off the lake this morning. "I was just checking to see if you need help bringing stuff out to the car."

She's got the paper boxes stacked neatly in the hallway. "Oh. Are you sure?" She pops her head around the doorframe from the living area. Her eyes sweep over me, and I straighten. I'm hurting today. All the wood chopping the other day is catching up with me, and I've been sleeping like shit. I haven't given myself a moment of rest while I beat myself up about abandoning our budding relationship.

"Yeah. Backseat?"

She nods and ducks away. I load the boxes one by one until there's almost no room left. Her suitcases will have to go in the trunk or the passenger seat because they won't fit back here.

With nothing else to do, I close the car door and go back inside, drifting through the rooms until I find Monica standing in the middle of her bedroom. She's holding one of my sweatshirts up to her face, and I'm not sure if she's sniffing it or deciding whether she should take it with her or leave it behind.

"You can keep it," I tell her, voice gruff with the swell of emotion at seeing her holding my clothing.

"Shit." She startles and almost drops it. "How are you so sneaky?"

I shrug my shoulders in a gesture of innocence. "Years of training?" She just shakes her head and stuffs the sweatshirt into her suitcase without remorse. "Are you going right away?"

She zips the bag closed before turning to face me, hands shoved into her jeans pockets. "I might as well. There's no food in my apartment, so I have to stop by the grocery store on the way home."

Monica's not the type to ask her assistant to do something like that for her, even if it makes her life more convenient. She's not even the type to reach out to her friends for help.

Everything about her tells me that she's not the type of woman who would stoop to her father's level.

Regret. Shame. Desperation. They all drive me forward.

Her eyes widen in surprise as I wrap my hands around her waist, sealing our lips together in a desperate kiss. She freezes for a second before going soft and pliant against me, fingertips resting against my sides in a tentative hold.

I want to pull her into me, imprint myself on her until she'll never be able to forget about me. It's too late to ask her to stay now, but maybe soon.

She pulls back, gasping for breath. Her cheeks are flushed a pretty pink that brings a savage sense of satisfaction to my ego. Soon enough, she regains her balance, and a steely determination hardens her eyes and straightens her spine. "This is not over between us, Caleb Corcoran."

"No, it's not." I shake my head. "I shouldn't ask you to wait for me."

"I will." She's all too willing to agree without knowing what else I'm going to say.

"Don't they teach you to wait for the terms first in lawyer school?" I tease.

"This is me giving you time and not asking questions you're not ready to answer." She steps into me this time, hands looping around my neck and pulling my face down for a much sweeter, softer kiss. "This is me saying I'll wait for you to figure your shit out and realize that we're good together."

"Even if sometimes you want to stab me." I'm half joking and half serious.

"Lately, it's been more fantasies of clunking you in the head with one of your freshly chopped chunks of wood. But yes. Even then."

I help her put on her coat and grab her suitcase over her protests. We walk out to her car, and I stow it in the trunk, lingering by the driver's door to help her inside. And maybe steal one more chance to touch her before she drives away.

She must be thinking the same thing because we step into each other at almost the same time. She wraps her arms around me in a hug and buries her face in the spot where my jacket gapes open.

"Call me when you're ready to talk?"

I nod. "I promise."

She looks sad, and I hate that I'm the one who made her feel that way. "I'll let you know when I make it home."

"Appreciate it."

I stand, holding the door frame, while she gets in and tucks her feet inside. I shove it closed and flinch at the sound of the engine turning over. My feet freeze in place as I watch her pull down the long driveway.

Fool.

For once, my head and my heart agree.

IT'S BEEN a week since Monica moved back to Green Bay. The weather has swung between late winter snows and afternoon thaws and left everything outside a swampy, muddy mess that just refreezes into treacherous ruts overnight.

Since I can't do much work outside, I've been fixing things up inside. When it gets dark or I need a break, I take care of clerical work.

Like sending Monica her bill.

It feels so final that I almost hope she won't pay it, but she does. Within three hours of receiving it. Damned efficient woman.

God, I miss her.

We've been texting off and on but shied away from anything serious. When she asked for pictures of Sherman, I tried to send one every day. I want to pick up the phone and call her, but I'm terrified she'll be working and I'll disrupt something important. Even the night seems off-limits since I know she works late and has been catching up with her family and friends.

Andrea sent me a picture of the two of them together last night, and Nore began prodding me for information.

Steve and Matt are stubbornly silent, but Bret came by a few days ago to hang out.

He was as bad as the ladies in trying to get me to come to my senses. Except I already have. I'm just not sure how to tell her everything she needs to know. Or if I even can.

Desperate for something to do, I get dressed and walk out to the mailbox. Usually I drive up, but I want the extra time outside of the house. Maybe the fresh air will clear my head and give me some much-needed perspective. Plus, I haven't checked it in a few days, so it's probably overflowing.

When I get to the box, I'm surprised to find a large, thick envelope shoved inside, along with the usual bills and junk mail. Pulling the mess out, I sort through it on the walk back.

I don't recognize the name or return address on the big envelope and move it to the bottom of the pile, pulling out junk mail and anything I know I can shred right away. Bills are a top priority, so I keep them separate.

Sherman's waiting for me at the door, sniffing the air before turning and sauntering toward my office. I follow him, toeing off my shoes off as I go. When I reach my desk, I toss the mail down before hanging my coat on the back of my chair and settling in to deal with the checks I need to write.

The giant envelope is last, and I rip it open with a deft pull. A stack of papers and a folder full of information comes out. I study the cover letter. Something about a grant and forms asking for more personal information and copies of my business plan.

The folder has information about the organization named on the front, and I glance over statistics and charts that detail data about veterans and their post-military careers.

What is all of this?

My brain can't make sense of the amount of money they're giving me or even why they're offering it in the first place. I shove it all back in the envelope it came in and set it aside to deal with tomorrow.

Sherman jumps up and sits on it, glaring at me like I'm an idiot. "I think I'm hallucinating. If you say something..." My sentence trails off, and I watch, worried that I've lost it.

He just sighs and lies on top of the envelope.

I WAKE up early the next morning and go straight to my office, taking all the papers out of the envelope. I read through them with more care, trying to stay open-minded about what they're telling me. For all I know, this could be an elaborate scam.

Except it doesn't seem like a scam.

From what I understand, I was accepted into a grant program for veterans who are starting their own business after leaving the military. But it doesn't tell me anything about why I got picked or how they even got my name.

Maybe someone from the support group has heard of them? There's a meeting this afternoon, and I could go down and ask around. Maybe it was even Dr. Black who nominated me.

With that plan in mind, I stay busy all morning, trying to get extra work done since I won't be home for a good part of the afternoon. When I get to Sturgeon Bay, I see fewer cars than the last time and get nervous that I'll stick out like a sore thumb. Or that I'll have to talk. I don't mind listening to everyone else, and it's nice being in a group of other veterans again, but I'm still not ready to talk about what happened yet in front of people.

Not before I've talked to Monica and we've figured something out.

One by one, people stand and speak, but no one seems to notice me beyond a cursory nod or handshake. After everyone's done, I stay for the coffee and snacks and try to slip the name of the grant into conversation to see if anyone's heard of it.

Finally, I find someone who has. The group leader, an older man named Greg, who also served in the Army, gets excited when I mention it. "You got one?" he asks, face surprised. "Those are scarce. Whoever wrote you that recommendation letter must have some connections. Especially to get it that fast."

"That's the thing. I don't know who might have done it." Maybe it was one of the guys?

He shakes his head, bemused. "Whoever nominated you must know someone who knows someone. Usually, you need a legislator's recommendation or at least something from a professional organization."

"Yeah." It's all I can get out because my mind's latched on to *legislator*. Monica. Did she do this?

I'm not sure what to think. Should I be offended that she thought I needed the help or glad to have her support? Either way, I need to talk to her about it. Since I'm halfway to her already, it makes sense to go down and see her. I might be able to catch her at the office. Less personal that way.

Anticipation gives me a lead foot, and I arrive outside of

her office faster than I should have. I spot Monica's car in the lot and park in a free space on the street. Grabbing the manila envelope, I head inside.

A pretty young woman, I'm guessing Alicia based on Monica's descriptions, is lingering at reception. She looks surprised to see me, and I wonder if Monica's told her about us. Her eyes widen, and her back straightens.

"Hi. How are you doing?" I paste on my customer service smile to look more friendly. I might be a little rough around the edges at the moment since I haven't bothered shaving in a few days and I'm still in my work clothes. Self-consciousness rattles through me.

"Hi. Can I help you?" She wrings her hands together, and her eyes dart down the hallway.

"Yes. I'm looking for Monica Price? If she's free, I'd like to speak with her." I hold up the envelope like that will explain everything.

"Let me go check." She gestures toward the sitting area. "Have a seat."

She hustles away, and I fold myself into one of the too-small chairs in the lobby. My knee bounces up and down with an acute case of nerves, and I freeze when I hear his voice down the hall. Then Monica's. Footsteps approach, and some instinct drives me to stand up and face whatever confrontation is coming.

Out from the hallway comes the frantic-looking woman I just met and Monica, with her head bent forward to listen to whatever another woman is whispering in her ear.

Followed closely behind Monica is Paul Price Senior. Immaculate in a three-piece suit even though he's officially retired.

Bile rises in my gut, and I clamp my mouth shut. Monica's eyes fly up to meet mine, an instant smile spreading across her beautiful face. It does nothing to put me at ease since the devil is standing right behind her.

"What are you doing here?" Paul Price's booming voice silences every other conversation in the office. "You're not sniffing around for more money, are you?" He puts on a front like he's offended, but I can see the calculation in his eyes.

"What?" Monica gasps, turning a horrified look at her father.

18

MONICA

"This is none of your business. Go back and wait in your office." My father is so used to being in charge and me obeying without question that he turns back to Caleb and ignores me.

The last pieces of respect I have for him fracture, and I feel like if I push too hard, they'll turn to ash. "I will not." I step around my father and move to Caleb's side. Caleb's eyebrows raise, and his body stills while my father turns a distinct shade of red. I've only seen it once or twice growing up when Paul or I did something so far out of line that he lost his temper.

Caleb glances between the two of us and half turns, so he's facing me with his back to my father. "I need to talk to you about something."

For the first time, I notice he's holding a thick manila envelope in his hands. "We can go to my office. I'm free now." I say the last part a little louder so my father will hear it and take a hint. It also gives me a little thrill of confidence to stand up to him for once in my life.

"We are not done." His face verges toward purple, and he turns his gaze from me to Caleb. I think about calling Mom because there's a distinct possibility he might have a heart attack. "And *you* will not be going anywhere with my daughter."

There's an edge of panic in his voice that gives me pause. Is Dad scared of him? I want to laugh at the thought of anyone being afraid of Caleb because it's so ridiculous. Caleb squeezes his eyes shut, and I notice how hard he's gripping the edges of the envelope. It sinks in that my father and Caleb might have some sort of history.

"Do you know my father?" I ask, low enough that Caleb's the only one who can hear me.

His jaw shifts as he grinds his teeth together. "We've met."

Unexpected relief fills me. Based on his reaction, Caleb is one of the few people who sees through Dad's public relations facade. "When?"

Caleb's mouth opens, but no words come out. His eyebrows pinch together, and my father is there, pushing between the two of us. "Monica, let me handle this. He's just after money. Nothing to concern yourself with."

"Why would he be after money?" I'm thoroughly confused at this point. Maybe Dad is confusing Caleb with someone else.

"Because I've already paid him off once."

My head whips toward my father in shock, and then I turn to Caleb. The questions I want to ask him die on my lips when I see he's gone pale. Tense. *Has he taken money from my father?*

"I'm sorry," Caleb says, face downcast. "I couldn't tell you. Technically, I still can't."

My brain feels frenetic. The need to make connections between what I'm seeing and hearing is so urgent that I can't focus on anything else. Caleb knew what an NDA was when I sent it to him. Was he livid because he signed one for my father before?

"Keep your mouth shut, and I'll give you the same amount," my father grinds out low enough that no one but Caleb and I can hear him. Alicia and Naia are watching from the hallway with concerned looks, and our receptionist is staring wide-eyed at the scene.

I keep puzzling over things, putting pieces into place. Caleb hates politicians. He hated me at first. Every time I took a call from my father in front of him, he tensed up.

"I'll never take another penny from you. Even if it means I lose everything," Caleb forces out through a clenched jaw, staring at my father with barely contained rage.

"Please." Dad scoffs. "Everyone has a price."

"He doesn't." My voice is firm, and I square my shoulders, standing side by side with Caleb. He tenses and then holds himself in a protective stillness, as if he's surprised I'm standing up for him again. In the fraught silence that lingers between the three of us, I watch as some of the fight leaves his posture.

"He has before. I'm sure we can come up with an acceptable number again." Now, Dad's switching into business mode.

"It was you, wasn't it?" Caleb told me a rough outline of what happened, but now I'm filling in the details. "You were there when Caleb was hurt. You covered everything up."

Dad's lips purse, and he looks irritated that I've figured it out. "That is none of your business."

"Except it is." I take a step forward, shifting so that I'm

partially in front of Caleb, not that I'll do much good at deflecting Dad's wrath when he aims it at him. "You can leave now. We're done here."

A flash of surprise makes him look human for a moment before determination takes it away. "We are not. Pull yourself together. People are watching."

"Then leave, because I have nothing more to say to you."

"Monica—" Caleb starts to speak, but I shake my head.

Dad opens his mouth to say something vile, I'm sure, but I cut him off.

"You should know that Naia was listening to our conversation on an open conference call line. If you don't leave immediately, I will have her inform the district attorney. I'm sure he'll be interested in learning how you're planning to intervene on Alana's behalf. Legally or otherwise."

Caleb stiffens at my back, and Dad goes still.

"You will also stop threatening me and trying to direct my career." I take a small step forward, getting closer to Dad's face and forcing him to step back. "And you *will* leave Caleb alone and not attempt to contact either of us for any reason unless we reach out first."

Dad opens his mouth, but Naia steps forward and cuts him off. "It's time for you to leave now, Mr. Price. Please have a good evening."

The presence of someone else, someone who's not family, snaps Dad to attention. He turns, grabs his coat from the rack, and storms toward the door. Naia meets him at the door, holds it open, and watches out the window as he walks to his car. Saying a silent prayer, I wish for him to drive away and lick his wounds at home, where he can do less damage.

I turn to face Caleb, but he looks shell-shocked. We should get out of here. It's close enough to the end of the day, and my father was my last scheduled meeting. If there's any work I need to catch up on, I can do it from home. "Come on. Let's go."

Caleb stares for a moment, but I gently grasp his hand, and he lets me tug him down the hallway toward my office. Once I close the door, I take a deep breath, savoring the moment of privacy before I collect my things and then drag him back up front. Naia eyes the two of us and gives me a look that says we'll talk about this later.

I lead Caleb to my car, unceremoniously shoving him into the passenger seat. We'll get his truck later.

"Where are we going?" he asks when I start the engine. The short sentence breaks the silence I've been afraid to breach.

"Back to my place."

When I get Caleb upstairs, I reach the end of the plan I concocted during the stand-off with my father. For once, I'm not sure what to do next. We need to talk about what just happened, but he still looks numb and didn't say more than a handful of words on the drive here.

"Why don't we sit on the couch?" I go to it, hoping he'll follow. He lingers in the entryway, looking around at my stark apartment. I try to see the space through his eyes. Compared to his cabin, it's light and empty. I've lived here for five years now, and it still looks close to how it did when I moved in.

"I came down to talk to you about this." He holds up the envelope he's still clutching like a lifeline. With labored movements, he pulls off his shoes and isolates himself in the farthest corner of the couch, staring across the room and clutching the envelope so hard the edges are wrinkled. "I'm sorry," he says.

"For what?"

He looks down at his hands and then away from me. "I'm a little... overwhelmed."

I think that may be the understatement of the century. "What can I do to help?" He looks so lost, I'm getting worried. The strong and assured Caleb I'm so used to seeing is nowhere to be found. For him to be this visibly shaken is concerning.

But also incredibly humanizing.

For so long, he's kept himself separate from everyone around him. It's a privilege to be the one he trusts enough to be there when his walls fall down.

19

CALEB

I don't know how to answer her. Too many thoughts are crashing through my head. Anger and hurt over seeing her father. Surprise that she stood up for me against him. Confusion about what she was talking about in the end that finally made him leave. And the mixed-up feelings of love and want I've been battling for months now.

"I'm not sure," I say when the silence has stretched out into an awkward band between us. "Do you mind if we just sit here for a minute?" Maybe that will give me enough time to sort out my thoughts.

"Of course." She scoots an inch closer and then restrains herself. "Will you just hold my hand or something?"

I turn to look at her and see she looks just as off-centered as I feel. When I hold my arm out, she burrows into my side. The restless part of me settles as I hug her close. I breathe in her familiar scent, absorbing her calming presence and feeling the steadiness she alone seems to grant me.

We sit up but stay close to each other. It's incredible how much I've missed her these last few days. "I think I understand why you hated me so much now," she says, voice quiet and careful.

"I don't think I ever hated you." No. Not hate. She confused me and made me feel things I didn't want to deal with. "But I heard you in the hospital hallway talking to him and—"

What are you going to do? Cover this all up and pay a few people off?

Her words from last spring echo in my mind, and I flinch.

"And I sounded like my father." It's a statement, not a question, but I nod anyway. "He's why you always acted differently after I got off the phone with him." Another nod.

We lapse into silence, and I wish I knew what to say. How to tell her how much I want and need her but how scared I am. "And I felt guilty about the accident. We were arguing, and I distracted you."

She squeezes my hand. "Truth be told, I don't think there would have been a different outcome if we were doing anything else. Evasive driving is not in my skill set."

"But still—"

"Caleb. It wasn't your fault."

I stare at her, letting her words sink into my bones. *What have I done to deserve her faith?*

We sit together, clinging to each other. No words are spoken, but my thoughts are still screaming at me. "What were you talking about just before he left?"

She turns into my side and tucks her head against my outer arm, hugging it close to her body. "Dad tried to bribe me to get me to do what he wanted. For once, I didn't want to just go along with his plans, so I set him up to get some leverage of my own."

"What'd he want you to do?" Something in me settles, knowing that she has something she can use against him now. For people like her father, power and leverage ran the world.

"Either run for my brother's seat in the state senate or line myself up to become a district attorney in a few years. He tried to make it sound like I had a choice." She sighs. "Neither was an option I wanted for myself, and I couldn't let Alana get off for what she did."

"He was going to get her a deal?"

"Yeah."

Another long silence.

"I got this in the mail today." I show her the envelope. She takes it from me, slipping the sheaf of papers out so she can look at them.

"Oh, wow," she breathes, surprise widening her eyes. "They worked fast."

"You applied for it?" I'm not mad at her for interfering or ashamed to need the help.

"Not fully. I just mentioned that you'd be an excellent candidate and that they should reach out." She looks up at me, excitement coloring her cheeks red. "This is a big deal, Caleb. They only give one or two of these out a year."

I love you. I love you. I love you. The words beat at my brain, demanding to be set free. My chest feels tight at her belief in me. Her obvious pride about me earning this grant. That other people see the same worth in me that she does.

"You're not mad, are you?" She shifts back, her smile fading when I just stare at her.

"I want to make this work," I blurt. "Between us, I mean.

I don't know how we're going to do it, but I think I love you, and I don't want to let you go."

She blinks in surprise, her cheeks turning even more red than they were before.

"That might have come out a little blunt." I can feel my own cheeks heat as she smiles.

"I already negotiated to go hybrid at work so I wouldn't have to be in the office every day. I wanted to tell you before I left, but then you were acting so weird, and I wasn't sure what to do."

I'm an ass. There's no way around that, but at least she still wants to put up with me.

"I'm sorry."

"Just try to talk to me more next time? And don't let my dad become an obstacle again."

"Promise me you'll keep giving me chances even when I don't deserve them?"

She leans close, taking my face in her hands and pressing a gentle kiss to my lips. "You always deserve another chance. Now, promise me you'll at least try not to push me away?"

Looking into her eyes, I feel the future spinning in front of me, bright and optimistic. All I can think about is how much I need her. "I promise. I know we'll have to see him from time to time—"

She cuts me off. "I'd prefer to avoid that about as much as you."

I grin, settling my hand on her thigh and wishing more than anything that we'll never have to deal with her dad again. "That went far better than I thought it would."

Her laugh is radiant and carefree. "Did you think I was going to slam the door in your face and throw a fit?"

"Honestly,"—I lean in, pressing her back into the couch and slowly crawling over her—"as long as I know you won't take off, I enjoy the occasional fight with you."

"Hmm." She bends her knees, and I settle against her. Thank god her couch is wider than mine. "And why is that?"

"Because at least then I know you care and think I can do better."

She melts beneath me. "We're going to work on this lack of belief in yourself." Her fingers trace up my arms. "But for now, will you please kiss me?"

"Gladly."

Nerves rattle through me, and I'm dreading what she might think. We've been driving back and forth to see each other for the last two weeks, and I've only just convinced her to leave some things here so she won't have to pack and unpack so much.

Sherman's been supervising me all morning while I rearrange the closet and clear out drawer space. Luckily, I don't have a ton of toiletries, so there are a couple of spare shelves in the bathroom.

She should be here soon.

In a rush, I change the sheets since they're looking wrinkly, and then hastily arrange the pillows so it looks like I am the stable, self-respecting adult I pretend to be. I don't know why I'm trying so hard since she's seen all this before and knows most of my habits by now.

Sherman's ears prick up, and he jumps off the bed, padding toward the front door.

I run my hands down my shirt, making sure it's tucked in

and as wrinkle-free as it can be. For once, I put on something other than a T-shirt, and the collared button-up feels like it's trying to strangle me. Needing some more air, I undo another button and roll up my sleeves to below the elbow.

The car door opens outside, and I rush after Sherman. The least I can do is help her carry whatever she's brought in. Knowing her, it'll be half a carload. I get the front door open just as she tugs out a suitcase from her trunk, and blessedly, it lands on a dry part of gravel. Early March is not a good time to be dragging things along on the ground.

"I'll get it." I rush forward and pick it up by the handle.

"Thank you." She looks harried, so it must have been a long day at work.

I take another bag from her when she pulls it out. Seeing my hands full, she shoulders her briefcase and grabs a file box. For the life of me, I don't know why she prints everything off since most of her work gets done online now.

Going ahead, I shoulder the door open so she can put her things down first. She makes a beeline for the office, dumping her work supplies on the temporary desk I set up for her last weekend.

I go to the bedroom, put her things on the bed, and step back, wiping my hands on my pants and looking around anxiously. *Shit, I forgot to light the candles.* One of the only personal things she has in her apartment is a massive collection of candles. I was worried about Sherman and his long fur, so I ordered a dozen of the flameless kind.

Remote. Remote. Where'd I put the remote?

I spot it on the bedside table and click the "On" button, hoping it's pointed in the right direction. A warm glow softens the room, and I sigh in relief.

"Mr. Corcoran, are you trying to seduce me?" Monica

teases from the door, and I spin, surprised she's snuck up on me.

"Is it working?" With her, I'm easily distracted in that direction, and it would definitely help assuage my anxiety if she were touching me.

"It worked a while ago." She steps inside and comes straight to me, putting her arms around my shoulders and kissing me. "But it looks very nice."

"Welcome home," I whisper, peppering kisses along her cheekbone and down her neck.

"I love you, Caleb." She moans, fingers gripping the back of my neck. "And you know you don't have to try this hard, right?"

I hum against her skin, fingers tugging up the hem of her cardigan. "For you, I'll always try this hard."

EPILOGUE

MONICA-MEMORIAL DAY

It's still pleasantly cool, thank god, because I'm sweating my butt off helping Caleb get everything ready for this party. His official grand opening for the bed-and-breakfast is tonight, and we've invited everyone. Andrea and Steve closed the restaurant for the night and are bringing most of their staff over. Even Sarah and Bret have their restaurant crew coming along with most of the guys from Bret's gym. Plus, almost every person we even passingly know responded positively to our invitation.

Everything has to go well, not only for Caleb's launch but also because he's meeting my brother and Grandma tonight. Mom and Dad were going to come, but then Mom got called into the hospital, and Dad stayed home. Caleb's only reaction when I told him was a small nod before hurrying away to get ready.

Personally, I'm relieved. While I would have liked to see Mom, I've avoided Dad for the last two months. There's only been a few phone calls and one forced family dinner breaking the no-contact streak.

"I told the caterers where to set up, and I think we've got decorations almost done." Alicia bustles by. She's carrying a case of tiny flags that we plan on handing out to everyone. We're having a memorial ceremony and a big party after that.

"Thank you. You really don't have to do all of this, you know."

"I want to." She smiles brightly and cheerfully in her red, white, and blue romper. "Besides. You've done so much for me, and I won't get to see you much longer."

When I went back to the office, Alicia decided to continue school and pursue her law degree. I wrote her letters of recommendation, and she's starting at UW Madison with a full-ride scholarship in the fall. I don't think she's aware, but I asked Paul to pull some strings for her, and he helped me set up the trust that's funding it. Alicia's smart, though, so I'm sure she suspects.

"Don't remind me." I grin and give her a quick side hug. The musicians are coming down the driveway, so I break away to let them know where to set up. We hired a semi-famous local band to play for the evening.

After I get them situated, I run into the house to check on the interior setup. Before I can actually check on anything, I'm pulled into the supply closet by a firm hand. I squeak but don't put up a fight. My body relaxes against Caleb, and he uses my compliance to pull me close.

"You looked like you needed a break," he murmurs close to my ear, shivers of awareness spreading across my skin.

"Or did you just want to seduce me in a closet?" My hand finds its way from his chest, tracing lines up and over his shoulder until I can cup his nape and pull him down for a kiss.

"Is that an option?" He steps closer to me, pressing my body against the shelves. I pray we don't knock things off. The noise would be enough for someone to come investigate.

"Not right now." My body aches with the need to be close to him. We've spent more time together than apart these last few months, and I still can't get enough of him. "But later..." I waggle my eyebrows.

"Please." He scoffs. "We're going to be so tired later, it'll be a miracle if we don't fall asleep standing up."

I laugh, pressing my face against his chest and shifting so I can loop my arms around his waist. "That's true."

"Your grandma here yet?" he whispers, keeping his voice low and skimming his lips along the shell of my ear, down my neck, and over my exposed collarbone.

"No." My breath quickens, and I arch upward. "But I think I just saw Matt and Nore pull up before I came in."

"What about your brother?" His fingers move over the light material of my sundress, subtly bunching it higher and higher.

"No." My voice is squeaky.

"Then we've got a little while longer, at least." His fingers slip under the edge of my underwear, and I widen my stance to give him more room. "Think you can be quiet, princess?"

"God, no," I groan.

He chuckles and brings his free hand up to cradle the back of my head, guiding my face against his chest to muffle the wanton noises already coming from me.

Caleb's fingers work in magical circles and thrusts. Faster than I ever believed possible, I'm coming apart in his arms. When I regain my balance, I straighten, putting a hand against his chest. My fingers make it to his pants button before he stops me, stilling my quest to give him the same release he just gave to me. “Not right now.” He dips his head and kisses my lips, my nose, and across my cheekbones. Featherlight brushes tease and deepen, turning into savoring pulls of lips and teeth and tongue.

“Why?” I whine.

From somewhere outside the closet, we hear, “The party has arrived!” closely followed by laughter and cheers.

Caleb raises his eyebrow in proof, and I pout. “Fine.”

His deep laugh rumbles out of him, and he smiles. “C’mon, before Ben catches us.”

Caleb’s hand settles on my lower back, and I push open the door. Ben’s barreling down the hallway with all his giddy, boyish energy. When he spots us, he yips in delight, diving in for a group hug.

“My two favorite antisocial workaholics. I still can’t believe you’re hosting such a big shindig, but man, I’m glad I could make it.”

“Watch who you’re calling a workaholic,” I tease. Ben’s thrown himself into his new role as a culinary instructor at a school in Chicago.

“At least this job comes with some delicious side perks.” He winks and is suddenly distracted by someone behind us.

I turn to find Daniel, Andrea’s sous chef, helping the caterers haul food in through the kitchen door. Ben watches him, and I raise an eyebrow in question. When Ben looks back at me, he scowls. “Have you seen Andrea and Steve yet?”

“They should be here soon.” I wonder if they know Ben has a thing for Dan.

Solar-powered string lights loop along the edges of the tent and into the main area. Even the lighthouse is lit up like a Christmas tree. Music reverberates across the property, and the party is in full swing. People are everywhere, including a few of the members of Caleb's old unit. Steve and Matt reached out to them to see if anyone might make it.

Paul and Lisa stick to the outskirts of the crowd, but Grandma and Caleb are in the middle of the dance floor, putting on a show. The pair hit it off right away. When he wasn't looking, Grandma gave me a big wink before stealing him away. He must like her too, because the pair of them have been showing off on the dance floor.

I linger near the back, watching the caterers to make sure they're getting a break when they need it and helping the servers clean up wherever I can. The band's going to be going for another hour at least, and I don't want to make everyone stay until the wee hours of the morning to help clean.

"Man, this place is nice," Naia says from next to me, and I preen at her admiration. This is all Caleb. He planned this and deserves all the praise he's getting.

"Caleb's done a wonderful job." I watch his and Grandma's antics while we speak.

"I don't want to pull you away from your duties, but can we speak for a moment?" Naia gestures around the side of the guest house, where there are fewer people and more privacy.

My gut swoops, knowing what she wants to talk about. "Of course."

She leads me into a private corner. "Has your dad been bothering you at all?"

With Alana's trial starting tomorrow, we're being extra careful to avoid any potential conflicts of interest. "No. He was supposed to come tonight, but he canceled at the last minute."

"Good. That's good." She reaches out and takes my hand. "I think the DA has a straightforward case against her and enough evidence to continue building convictions on the other cases, but it's still likely that you'll be called to testify early on. Are you ready for that?"

I swallow and squeeze her hand. "I think the odds are low, but yes, I'm ready." We've done some prepping about things they might ask me, but I'm not worried.

"If you need anything, I want you to ask, alright? You've been doing so well these last two months. I don't want you to get overworked again."

"I will. I promise." Since I've moved to the hybrid schedule, I've felt much more balanced, and I'm able to enjoy the work I'm doing again. Naia's been great about letting me pick what projects to focus on and take the lead with.

We move out of the shadows, and I glimpse Ben leading Daniel off somewhere. I shake my head and smile, used to his antics by now. A new couple has taken over center stage on the dance floor, and my eyes automatically scan the crowd, searching for Caleb.

"I'll talk to you later?" I ask Naia when I spot him over by the lighthouse's utility door.

"Of course." She chuckles and says something that sounds like "young love" as she moves back into the fray.

Caleb sees me coming and nods toward the door. We kept it locked today so it wouldn't tempt anyone to go up to the top floor while they were drinking. The spiral staircase is a doozy even when you aren't tipsy.

When I reach him, Caleb unlocks the door, and I dart inside. By mutual agreement, we make our way upstairs. From here, we can see the crowd and hear the thumping music, but the noise is dampened by the glass, making it easier to hear each other speak.

"How are you holding up?" I ask, cuddling against his side. Crowds and noise are still not his favorite things, so this has to have been a lot for him. Combined with the stress of hosting and seeing his old friends, I'm sure he's overwhelmed.

"I'm better now." He presses a kiss on the top of my head. We stand together without speaking for a few minutes, just letting our batteries recharge. "I think your grandma likes me."

I snort. "I didn't know you could dance like that."

"I didn't either." He tugs me close and loops his arms around me. "Tonight's gone well."

"You did a fantastic job. Looks like a great start to your first year in business." I lean back so I can look him in the eye. "I hope you know how amazing you are. No matter what, you've worked hard to start this business, and that's not something most people are willing to do."

Instead of shying away from the praise, he gives me a quick nod of acknowledgment. "You've helped me so much to believe in myself."

"You would have done this without me." I poke a finger into his chest. "Admit it."

"Eventually. But not this quickly." He smiles and ducks in for a kiss. "I love you, princess."

"I love you too, Caleb."

We linger in silence a little longer. "You want to head back down to the party?"

He grunts in denial. “Can we stay up here until everyone leaves?”

“No.” I settle one of his hands at my waist and grasp the other. “But we have a few minutes. Dance with me?”

The band is playing a slower tune. “Whatever you ask for, I’ll always give you.” We sway together, and when the song ends, we keep moving, our steps matching in an effortless flow.

APPRECIATION

It's hard to believe this is the final, full-length book in the Door County Dreams series. In some ways it's been the most difficult to write.

Befitting their stubborn personalities, Monica and Caleb's story did not reveal itself right away, and I struggled for months to get them to talk to me. This was not the experience I had with the first four books, so I was very nervous I wasn't going to get this one out at all!

Finally I remembered where this series began and how I felt writing that first short story that kicked off Matt and Lenore's romance.

After attending a writing retreat with James Mihaley at Write On Door County in 2017, I decided to take a massive leap and write a full-length book with the intention of self publishing. I was full of ambition and eager to explore that feeling of sending a book out into the world. That book, *Five Days in July,* took me almost three years to finish, and I was finally able to release it in July of 2022.

What a whirlwind it's been since then! In the last eighteen months, I've written five full-length novels, two novellas, four anthology contributions, and wrote and illustrated a children's book.

I never would have done any of those things without the spark that was kindled at that retreat. So thank you, Jim and Write On Door County for helping me take that initial leap!

Jill, I also need to thank you for your complete faith and enthusiasm in my journey. One conversation : to another and it led to me setting up my author account on Amazon and taking that chance at finally publishing my book.

Linda, Wendy, Amber, you've been incredibly supportive friends throughout this whole publishing process.

Dallas, Jen, Devin, and all of the other ARC readers who took a chance on a very new author and jumped in mid series, thank you! Your input and thoughts have helped me become a better writer and I hope to keep giving you stories that you love for many years to come!

And finally, my family, especially my father, has been endlessly supportive. Thank you for giving me the space and opportunity to do something as crazy as decide to publish a book, and then another and another and another.

ABOUT THE AUTHOR

Cecelia Conway is a romance author based in southern Wisconsin.

She loves creating characters and losing herself in imaginary worlds, whether as a writer or an avid reader.

A graduate of the University of Wisconsin Madison, she holds a BA in English/Creative Writing and a BS in Agriculture from Oregon State University.

Away from the keyboard, she works in special education and volunteers with several nonprofit organizations. Her favorite hobbies include reading, spending time with her cats, horseback riding, and photography.

Her debut series, *Door County Dreams*, is a five-book series of contemporary, small-town romance novels set in Door County, Wisconsin.

ALSO BY CECELIA

Door County Dreams:

Five Days in July

Four Weeks in September

Three Months in Spring

Two Nights in August

One Winter in Door County

2 Year Anniversary Novella: Coming July 2024 in the Total Fireworks Anthology

Capitol Shorts:

Bridging the Divide

Battling the Bureaucracy

Continued on next page...

ALSO BY CECELIA (CONTINUED)

Apostle Island Anomalies:

Saving the Selkie—Fall 2024

Waking the Wulver—Winter 2024

Playing the Pooka—Spring 2025

Book 4—Summer 2025

Taylor Sisters Trilogy :

Ring Sour: 2025

Barn Sour: 2025

Buddy Sour: 2025

BOOK LINKS
BLURBS &
CONTENT WARNINGS

Consider signing up for my newsletter to never miss a new release!

NEWSLETTER
SIGN UP

ONE WINTER IN *Door County*

CECELIA CONWAY

FIND CECELIA CONWAY ON SOCIAL MEDIA

Facebook:

https://www.facebook.com/ceceliaconwayauthor

TikTok:

www.tiktok.com/t/ZTd3xmEho/

Instagram:

www.instagram.com/ceceliaconwayphotography

Website:

www.ceceliaconway.com

BookBub:

https://www.bookbub.com/authors/cecelia-conway

Goodreads:

https://www.goodreads.com/ceceliaconway

Pinterest:

https://www.pinterest.com/ceceliaconwayauthor

Made in the USA
Columbia, SC
18 November 2024